TRAPPED
ON A CLOUD

TRAPPED ON A CLOUD

Phyllis Roth Lewis

CONTENTS

For my sisters: Marilyn, Sharon, Carol, Nyla,
Rhonda, and Kathy,
And our brother, Bill

CHAPTER 1

PETE

Pete was unhappy. What had he gotten himself into? Perhaps—if he were lucky—he was only dreaming, and soon he would wake up at home. Not really anything too wonderful to look forward to—a small apartment in an ugly part of Wichita; but at least he would get to see his mom and his brothers and sisters.

He sighed sadly and spread the fingers of his right hand upon the softness of the surface beneath him. He studied his hand as if he had never seen it before. Today the cloud was kind of gray-looking instead of its usual bright whiteness. Even so, his hand looked very dark against it.

Frowning, he pushed his hand hard, making it disappear into the strange stuff up to his elbow. Weird! Really weird! It made his arm feel cool and damp.

He pulled his hand back out. Some of the white fluff clung to his fingers. It felt like the hair mousse his mom used on her hair. Pete rubbed it around in his hand until nothing was left except some wetness.

Sighing again Pete adjusted his thin, lanky body a little more comfortably. Then he allowed himself to remember for about the hundredth time how he had ended up on this cloud-like place. Totally impossible, yet here he was.

It had all started on the broken, concrete steps in front of the apartment building where he lived. He had been sitting a couple of steps from the bottom holding his most prized possessions, a baseball and mitt. To amuse himself he had invented a game. The idea was to toss the ball a little higher into the air each time and then catch it without having to move his body.

The whole thing was all coming back to him like a rerun on television.

It had been late evening and almost dark—time to go get his little sisters and make them go inside. His mom wouldn't be getting home from her work shift until ten o-clock, and both his older brothers were out. Jim was at his new job, and Justin—well who knew where Justin was. Justin was sixteen and seemed to disappear every evening with his friends.

That night Pete had had complete responsibility for the two youngest members of the family, eleven-year-old Marianne and eight-year-old Joni.

Pete's mind continued to dredge up memories. He remembered exactly how it had all happened. In his mind he was now back there on the steps tossing his ball up into the air.

Pete missed the ball on his twenty-second toss. It hit the edge of his mitt, landed with a thud, and rolled away. He dived for it pretending he was retrieving a hard hit to the shortstop. He scooped it up and whirled around to tag out the runner.

Much to his surprise his mitt brushed against a very real leg. Gasping he yanked his mitt back. He clutched the mitt to his chest as he stared up from his crouching position at the lady attached to the leg.

She was standing there watching him with an amused expression. Her lips were painted deep red, her eyes outlined in thick, black lines, and her eyelids totally covered with a blue-green color. Although her skin was dark it wasn't black like his, but her hair was. It was very black. She had bangs down to her eyebrows with the rest of it hanging straight and shiny down her back.

Pete gulped, not knowing what to say to such a strange and beautiful creature.

Her amused look shifted to a smile of pleasure, and she said, "Hello, is this where you live?" She gestured toward the building.

Embarrassed by his ugly home he answered timidly, "Yes, ma-am."

"Do you like it here?"

What a stupid question, Pete thought. How could anyone like living in such an unpleasant place? He answered truthfully, "No, ma-am. It's ugly and dirty, and we've only got a small, two bedroom apartment on the top floor."

"Ah, yes. I suppose you would like to live somewhere clean and beautiful."

Pete ducked his head and sat back down on a step hoping the strange woman would leave, but she didn't. She also sat down, and so close to him that he felt funny. She smelled like some kind of flower—a nice smell, but still he didn't like her that close. He scooted away.

She smiled at him, her glittering green eyes inviting him to smile back, but he didn't. He didn't like her smile, and he didn't like the look in her eyes. It made him feel very, very weird.

"What is your name?" she asked in a low, husky voice.

"Pete Jones," he answered politely.

"Hello, Pete Jones. How would you like to go somewhere beautiful?"

Pete turned away from her hypnotic eyes and mumbled something about needing to be here when his mom got home from work.

"How many people live in your small, two-bedroom apartment?" she asked in an interested voice.

"I got two brothers and two sisters and my mom. My dad's not around no more."

"Pete, you look like a bright, young man. You are about thirteen or fourteen, I would guess."

He mumbled, "I'm thirteen." He made the mistake of looking her in the eyes. Then he couldn't seem to make his own eyes pull away. Hers were lit up with something he couldn't figure out.

She continued in a soothing tone, "Pete, I have been sent to find some special people to go to a beautiful place."

Suspicion flooded his mind, and he said rudely, "Get real, Miss. What are you trying to do? I'm not stupid enough to fall for no trick. What are you really up to? You pushing drugs?"

Her laughter rang through the air, "Now, Pete, do I look like a drug pusher?"

"No, but you got weird clothes, and your face looks like a painting of some Egyptian queen I saw in a museum."

"Pete, I promise you I am not trying to get you to take any thing. It is just that you looked so unhappy sitting on these steps, and I have been sent by a special person to look for unhappy kids."

"Why?"

"Because he cares very deeply for kids who deserve a better way of life."

Pete was still suspicious, but he couldn't tear his eyes away from hers, and her voice was so pleasant to listen to, and she smelled so nice—kind of like some lilacs his teacher had brought to school, but not quite. This was more spicy . . .

She broke into his thoughts. "Well, Pete, what about it?"

"Oh no, ma-am. I told you I have to be here when my mom gets home. You see, my little sisters are playing down the street, and I need to be here."

Her face lit up with joy and gave no sign of the lie she was telling. "But Pete, that is where I have come from. Your sisters are waiting for you."

"Why didn't they come home and get me?"

"I am sorry, but they were having such a good time I hated to make them leave."

Pete was bewildered. What should he do? He was responsible for Marianne and Joni. Maybe he should go get them. Something was up, and he had to take care of them.

It was fairly dark by now. Weak street lights at the corners were on, but they seemed more like small, far-off stars—not the bright, safe lights he was used to. What was wrong with them?

Suddenly, Pete was anxious. Something felt wrong. He stood up. "I'd better go check on my sisters," he said almost as much to himself as to the woman next to him.

"Of course," the woman answered, "It is rather dark now. I will walk with you to show you where they are."

Pete didn't say anything. He didn't know what to say.

They walked down to the corner and turned right, but when they reached the house where he thought his sisters were the strange woman touched his arm and said, "This way."

She led him toward a house that had been vacated years ago and was falling to ruin.

Pete heard children's excited voices coming from behind the house and felt relieved. Surely the strange woman was right about his sisters. It sounded like many of the neighborhood children were playing together.

Silently they both walked around to the rear of the house.

Pete stopped in surprise. What was that huge, black shape looming ahead? It looked a lot like a huge bubble.

Pete wasn't sure what he was seeing because of the dark, but he definitely wasn't seeing any kids. He could hear them, though. Their voices were coming from the big bubble thing—whatever it was.

The woman took him firmly by the arm and guided him toward the strange object. He didn't resist. He had to find his sisters.

Light was shining from a narrow opening in the side of the object. The woman gently pushed Pete through the opening.

Inside there were happy, excited kids. He looked for Marianne and Joni.

The woman continued to hold his arm. She led him over to a tall, handsome man and said gaily, "Nica, this is Pete."

The man smiled pleasantly. "How do you do, Pete. Glad to have you aboard."

Squeals and shouts brought Pete's thoughts back to the present. He glanced over at the group of kids romping around but wasn't in the mood to join them. Instead, he shifted his position so that now he was lying on his stomach with his head hanging over the side of the cloud. He stared down at the Earth below.

CHAPTER 2

PETE HELPS

Gazing down at the tops of trees and grassy fields Pete was thankful that his sisters had not been among the kids in the huge bubble. Jezbeel had lied to him about that. They were safely at home.

He wondered what his family was thinking about him. Did they think he had run away? Did they think he had been hurt? He wanted to cry, but he wouldn't. He had cried that first night but not since. He had to be tough.

The cloud drifted over a farmhouse, and he could see a man standing in his yard looking up at them.

Impulsively, Pete waved and almost shouted. Luckily, he caught himself in time. He had already been in trouble once for attempting to contact another human. Besides, the man was a very long way down there and would never hear him, but Nica or one of the others up here would.

Another Human! Pete thought bitterly to himself. Was he even a human any more? Somehow he doubted it, although he did not really feel any different than he ever had. He still thought like a thirteen-year-old human boy. Well, that was not exactly true. He now missed that daily trudging to Wichita Junior High School which, until a few weeks ago, he had hated with a passion. Who would ever have guessed that he would miss school as much as he missed hot fudge sundaes and Pepsi Cola and Pizza and . . .

Stop that, Pete told himself and concentrated once again on the man still staring up at them—or rather up at the cloud. The man below could not possibly see that there were humans hidden on the cloud. For some reason (a total mystery to him) Pete could now see farther than people on earth could. Must be something about the treatments they had to take to survive up here.

Pete could not really see the man's face all that well, but somehow he was positive the man was sad. He was also positive he was a farmer and was sad because the crops he had planted in his fields needed rain and needed it badly.

Without even attempting to stop himself he slid down the side of the cloud headfirst until he was at the bottom of it. Then he tightened his body and began plunging and diving and twisting his stiff-as-a-board body in and out of the lower part of the cloud. Faster and faster he flung his weight. The faster and harder he moved the happier he felt. Soon he was grinning, and by the time drops of rain began falling from the cloud he was laughing out loud.

He paused in his activity to look back down and was rewarded with a look of happiness on the distant farmer's face, or so he imagined. He could not make out the man's features, but he did think that anyone jumping up and down and swinging arms around like crazy had to be smiling.

Pete returned to the top of the cloud. He laughed happily at the sight of the rain falling upon the dancing figure below.

"Who's responsible for this?" a loud, deep voice demanded.

Pete's laughter died in his throat. He looked around him. There was now a crowd of kids, and in the midst of them stood Nica.

Pete stared at the man unable to force any words out of his mouth.

Nica was tall and muscular and very handsome in spite of the two-inch, jagged scar running down his right cheek. But now his good looks were twisted into ugliness, and the scar glistened white against his angry, red face.

For the first time Pete felt afraid of the man.

Pete looked into Nica's eyes, and instantly the man's face softened into the more familiar pleasant look he usually wore. However, he repeated his question in a stern voice, "Who made it rain?"

Many pairs of eyes turned on Pete, and he knew he was doomed.

He pulled himself up and reluctantly made his way over to Nica. "I'm sorry, Nica, but they needed rain bad. Surely it . . ."

He was interrupted, "Pete, it is not for you to decide. Who do you think you are? God?"

Ashamed, Pete ducked his head. He stared at his dirty sneakers and mumbled, "No, Sir. I'm sorry, Nica."

But Nica ignored his apology. Instead the big man yelled over his shoulder, "Sadju, come here."

Immediately a small, olive-colored man appeared by his side. Not only was he a foot shorter than Nica he was about half as big around. And where Nica was clean shaven Sadju had a shaggy beard, a thick mustache, and really bushy eyebrows which left only a small portion of his face exposed. This portion contained small round eyes, a large hooked nose, and a mouth full of crooked yellow teeth. Messy brown hair hung down to his shoulders.

Sadju was the ugliest person Pete had ever encountered, and the boy could not help but be fascinated by such complete ugliness.

Sadju asked in a soft, whiny voice, "What do you wish, Nica?"

"Get everyone together. I need to speak to everyone," the taller man commanded.

"Even the ones finishing up with Jez-beel? She won't like that, especially since there will be more work because of the rain."

"Do I care what Jez-beel thinks?' Nica asked arrogantly. "If she complains, I will have to have a talk with her, also. Now, get them all together."

"Yes, Nica," Sadju agreed, an oily smile upon his lips and malice in his tone. Instantly he disappeared.

Pete blinked. He knew these people (or were they creatures from another planet) were able to do remarkable things, but it still caught him off guard.

Nica's voice stopped any further speculations. "You, who are already here, sit down."

CHAPTER 3

KAYA AND VONNIE

Nica's voice demanding that they sit down quieted the excited murmuring of the kids.

Pete sank into a sitting position.

Brice, who had been a bully on earth, had attempted to continue his behavior here in their new world. With a mean look on his face he sat down beside Pete and whispered snidely. "Now, see what you've got us into." He made a fist and shook it at Pete. "If you don't straighten up I'll use this on you."

Pete stared into Brice's hard, blue eyes and said wearily, "Go ahead, Brice. I don't care."

The bully pulled back his arm, but a hand on it caused it to pause in midair. He twisted around to look into the face of the person who had arrived so quietly to spoil his fun. His face flushed at the sight of the tall girl whose hand was gripping his arm. Brice pulled his arm away from her grip and dropped his fist into his lap.

Brice scowled as he turned away from Kaya. He found himself looking directly into blue eyes very like his own but without any hardness or meanness. They belonged to a pretty girl who had seated herself next to Pete. Besides lovely, blue eyes Vonnie had curly, blonde hair and perfect features. She stared back at Brice but said nothing.

The first girl, the tall one with intelligent brown eyes, spoke as she settled down onto the ground between the two boys, "Brice, you do know that you can't bully anyone with that fist here, don't you?"

As Brice continued to scowl Pete wondered how anyone only twelve years old could sound as in charge as Kaya did. He was embarrassed. He should have handled the bully by himself instead of needing a girl to bail him out.

The only saving point was the instant knowledge that Brice also was feeling Kaya's impact for he muttered sheepishly, "Well, he'd just better straighten up or all of us will suffer." Then in a pleading tone he added, "Don't you understand that?"

Brice heaved his large, powerful body up and moved over to a group of kids who were seated close to where Nica had remained standing.

Nica was conversing with this group, and the look on his face was angelic.

Pete studied the man's face for an instant before turning back to Vonnie and Kaya. At their accusing looks he burst out, "I know. I was bad, but I just don't see what the big deal is."

Vonnie smiled, which caused dimples in her cheeks and sparkles in her sky blue eyes. She said, "Pete, don't you want to get off this cloud and go where we can live forever with everything we've always wanted?"

"Of course, Vonnie, but I couldn't help it. That man needed rain?"

"How do you know that?" asked Kaya in a curious tone.

"How did I know it?" he asked aloud with a questioning frown upon his face.

His expression smoothed out as he stated honestly, "I'm not sure, Kaya. It was just there—in my mind. You know, it's really strange. I mean, my knowing. I've never been on a farm, and the only thing I know about crops is what I've read in my social studies book."

A puzzled expression spread all over his face as he began wondering how he had known.

Vonnie's melodic voice floated into his thinking, "How did you make it rain, Pete?"

"And that's another thing," he started off, still amazed at himself. "How did I know I could move my body the way I did in the bottom of the cloud? How did I know that would make it rain?"

Pete stared at Vonnie's own puzzled expression. She was looking at him as if she had never seen him before. He turned to Kaya and asked her, "Have you noticed that you know things you didn't know before?"

Kaya frowned, then shook her head, "No, not exactly."

"What do you mean not exactly?" Pete asked.

"Well, I have noticed that when I have something to say people seem to stop and listen to me, and when I come up to people they stop whatever they're doing and kind of wait for me to say something." She paused, laughed merrily and admitted, "Gosh, that certainly sounds big-headed, doesn't it?"

Vonnie broke in, "No, you're right. I just figured you'd always been that way. Weren't you when you were back down on Earth?"

Kaya replied earnestly, "I always voiced what I thought, but no, back there no one paid all that much attention to what I said. What about you, Vonnie? Do you know things you didn't before?"

"Only that I seem to know how to do the cloud, you know, when it's my turn to help Jez-beel. Sometimes, I have to show some of the other kids where to put the cloud stuff."

Pete laughed, "You mean, it's not just me who doesn't get it? I don't ever have a clue about where to put that stuff. I'd just start piling it any old place if somebody didn't tell me any different."

Kaya shook her head slightly as if trying to shake something out of it and said solemnly, "Pete, we're different up here. I don't understand any more than you do, but I do know I don't want to stay on this cloud forever, so please, for the rest of us, won't you try to obey the rules?"

Pete shrugged his shoulders before folding himself into a position with his chin resting on his knees. He didn't say it aloud but wondered to himself once again. What had he gotten himself into? What had they all gotten themselves into?

CHAPTER 4

RULES

Soon all thirteen children and three adults were assembled. Sadju stood a little behind Nica. Jez-beel was as beautiful as ever but had a sullen look on her face as she lounged carelessly to the right of the men.

Pete could hardly keep his eyes off Jez-beel's perfect beauty. There was something hypnotizing about her. Her skin was smooth and brown. Her black hair hung straight down her back past her waist. Her face had not a single flaw. Her slim figure was outlined in a long, white, clinging garment.

She caught him staring at her and smiled.

Pete jerked his eyes away. He didn't like her smile. It reminded him of something—he couldn't say exactly what—but it was something that gave him a bad feeling.

Just then Billy Fred and Jo Jo joined them. Jo Jo always seemed to be grinning, and he greeted Pete in a sparkling tone to match his grinning mouth. "Don't worry. Be happy," the small, oriental boy advised merrily.

Pete groaned, shifted his attention away from Jo Jo and looked into Billy Fred's unusual face. It was unusual because all of the parts of it were large. His mouth was wide and his nose long. His eyes were set far apart and almost hidden under the droopiest eyelids Pete had ever seen except maybe on a basset hound. Above the eyes were really bushy eyebrows which were the same, sandy color as the hair that flopped down over his forehead.

Billy Fred pushed Pete over and dropped down to the ground between him and Vonnie. He said, "It's okay, Pete."

Pete gave Billy Fred a feeble smile but didn't have a chance to say anything. The other boy had already turned to Vonnie and was saying, "Hey, Vonnie, how can you confuse a blonde?"

Not giving her a chance to answer Billy Fred announced importantly, "Give her a bag of M&M's and tell her to put them in alphabetical order."

Pete could not help but laugh at the joke and at Vonnie's indignant look.

Nica's voice broke into their laughter.

Instantly, they quieted.

Nica said "It has been rudely brought to my attention that there is not a clear understanding of the rules here."

Pete felt his face sag. Nervously he pushed at the black curls covering his head, continued staring at Nica, and waited for the tall man to attack.

But Nica did not even look at him. Instead he said to no one in particular, "I fear that we are in for a long journey if we don't all get things straight. Therefore, I felt it imperative that we review what we are doing here and what we must—I wish to emphasize the MUST—do in order to move on to a better life." He paused, smiled pleasantly, and then turned to look straight into Pete's eyes.

Pete felt sick. He dropped his gaze and didn't look back up until Nica asked another boy a question in a voice of pure honey, "Owen, are you glad to be here?"

"Yes, Nica. I'm very glad to be here."

"Why?" Nica demanded in his pleasant voice.

Owen was a handsome, twelve-year-old with brown wavy hair, brown eyes, even features, and well groomed hair. He answered with no hesitation, "My life was awful. No one cared about me. I probably would have ended up on drugs."

He stopped and looked at Nica as if waiting for a cue.

Nica, however, turned to another boy, "Lennie, what about you? Are you glad to be away from your old life?"

Lennie turned sad eyes directly onto Pete.

Pete cringed, knowing all the kids were blaming him for this meeting. He deserved it. None of the other kids ever seemed to disobey one of the few rules they had.

Lennie was a slight, sickly boy with light brown hair, hazel eyes, and a mouth which was usually turned down. He spoke softly, "I'm very glad to be here. I know that some day I can throw these things away." He lifted two crutches which lay in front of him.

Pete caught a look of contempt on Jez-beel's face. He frowned, trying to figure out what was causing the lady's expression. She sensed his look and once again smiled at him. Quickly he glanced back at the boy speaking.

"I had a bad life before. I was always teased and picked on, and even my parents didn't like me. Thought I was a bother." Lennie's voice was heavy with bitterness.

"Pete, what about you?" Nica asked suddenly.

Pete's body jerked involuntarily. Nica had managed to catch him off guard. Pete glanced at Jez-beel. Her eyes were narrowed, and her expression seemed to be sending him a warning. He knew why. She had tricked him into coming to this place. She had gotten him into the bubble, and it had taken off while he had been looking for his sisters. Should he tell on her?

Pete moistened his lips. He wanted to shout out the truth, but somehow he knew he must not. He didn't know how he knew. It was like with the man below and the rain. He knew it, but he didn't know how he knew it.

Gathering his wits together he lied, "Yes, Nica, I'm glad to be here." Out of the corner of his eye he saw Jez-beel relax. He didn't relax, though. He felt awful. He hated the lie.

"You want to stay with the others when they go on to the new world?" Nica asked him.

"Yes, sir, I do." What else could he say?

"Then, Pete, you do realize that there are certain rules we must obey if we are to ever get there."

"Yes, sir," he admitted while at the same time wished the man would leave him alone, which miraculously he did.

Nica was now addressing the girl sitting beside Pete, "Kaya, you are an intelligent girl. I am sure you can remind all of your peers of our rules."

Pete thought there was an undertone of malice in the man's pleasant voice. He wished he could figure out what Nica was up to. There was something not quite right about the man.

Kaya stood up before answering, "Yes, Nica. There are only three."

Nica nodded encouragingly.

Kaya continued, "First, we must all take treatments twice a day."

"And why is that, Gene?" Nica asked of a small, ten-year-old boy sitting off by himself.

The boy looked at him with round, fearful eyes but said nothing.

"Come, Gene, you do know, don't you?"

The boy shook his head, causing his tangled mop of black hair to bob up and down, but said nothing.

"Cat got your tongue?" Nica asked smoothly.

The boy's head bobbed up and down again. His face was fearful, and he looked as if he would burst into tears.

"Oh, all right, I'll leave you be for now. Kat, perhaps you can help our young friend out."

Pretty mean, Pete couldn't help thinking. He knew Gene was extremely timid, and that it was like rubbing salt in a wound to ask the only child smaller than Gene to answer for him.

Kat was only eight years old—cute, cuddly, and not the least bit shy. She babbled happily most of the time, and the rest of the time she continued talking, although most often it was to tattle on someone else about something not in the least important. She recited prettily, "If we don't have our treatments we'll die."

"Yes, Kat, that is right. Do you remember that we had to take treatments in our space vehicle before I let you come out onto the cloud?"

The little girl nodded and said, "Yeah, and I remember we had to stay shut up in the bubble for a long time."

"Right again, Kat. We must continue the treatments daily. They keep us all alive and healthy and able to live in this atmosphere and with no food or water. It makes us superhuman."

Nica paused to once again catch Pete's eye, but quickly shifted his attention to Brice and asked, "Brice, isn't it nice to be a superhuman?"

"Yes, Nica," the bully answered enthusiastically.

"Would you ever think of missing your treatment?" Nica asked.

"No way," Brice answered. "I don't want to die."

"Exactly. It is important. Is there anyone here who does not agree that it's important?"

No one answered. That is, until Pete asked cautiously, "How do we know we would die if we missed a treatment?"

Nica looked amused as he asked his own question, "Don't you believe me?"

Luckily, as a black kid, Pete's embarrassment could not be detected. He answered as he knew Nica wanted him to answer, "Yes, Nica, I do. I was just wondering."

"Sometimes it is dangerous to wonder." Then with a malicious look he asked, "Pete, would you like to try going without a treatment?"

Vonnie gasped, and Pete felt some of his friends tense up, so he resisted the urge to answer defiantly. Meekly he replied, "No, Nica. I don't want to miss a treatment."

"I thought not," the man responded.

CHAPTER 5

THE SECOND RULE

"Now, Kaya, tell us the second rule," Nica said with a condescending smile at the standing girl

In a firm voice Kaya stated, "We must all do the work we are assigned to do."

"That is right. Vonnie, suppose you tell us what work that is."

Vonnie hopped up beside Kaya and explained, "Each day we're assigned to Sadju or Jez-beel to help them."

"What do you do when you help Sadju?"

Vonnie said in her clear, sweet voice, "Some of us help run the machines which make the material we use to form our cloud, and some of us take the material to the places where it's needed.

"Very good, Vonnie. Now, Jo Jo, suppose you tell us what you do when you help Jez-beel."

Jo Jo stayed seated as he answered with laughter in his voice, "We apply the material all over the cloud."

"And why do we do that?"

"For fun? To keep us amused?" Jo Jo answered in a questioning tone.

A look of irritation swept over the man's face but was instantly gone. However, his voice still retained some of his irritation as he said, "Of course not. Whatever gave you that idea?"

Jo Jo shrugged his shoulders and assumed a bewildered look, but Pete was sure that the boy was deliberately baiting their leader. Wondering why Pete decided to seek out the boy at a later time. Maybe Jo Jo would understand his own doubts about Nica and this strange place.

"Polly, help Jo Jo out. I believe he needs it." Nica's tone was once again smooth and pleasant.

Polly was as pretty a girl as Pete had ever seen, except, of course, for Jez-beel, which didn't count because she was old, and Polly was only twelve. But still Polly was pretty, even prettier than Vonnie. However, Pete didn't like Polly. She used her looks to get others to do things for her, and she was cruel sometimes.

Looking like an angel Polly treated Jo Jo to a scornful laugh.

The mean laughter was lost on Jo Jo though, for he seemed not in the least bit upset. He smiled warmly at the girl as if he would hang on to her every word.

Pete frowned to himself again as he took his eyes off the oriental boy to watch Polly respond to Nica's request.

"Jez-beel has us add some material every day because it only lasts for twelve to fourteen hours." Polly paused and smiled prettily at Nica and then added, "We don't want anyone to know we're here."

Nica nodded with approval at her.

She took this as an encouragement to go on. "We also form new shapes so people below won't suspect anything funny about our cloud since it doesn't always act exactly like a normal cloud would." She laughed again

Pete wanted to put his hands over his ears. He didn't like her laugh. Then it dawned on him as he automatically looked over at Jez-beel. Polly reminded him of the older woman. Her laugh and Jez-beel's smile were the same. Always at someone's expense. It made them both happy to see others embarrassed or upset. How awful! It seemed almost evil.

Pete forced himself to look down at his feet. What thoughts he was having—thoughts about evil. He felt someone studying him. He glanced up at Kaya who was standing in front of him and caught her eyes upon his face.

She leaned down toward him and mouthed, "It's okay, Pete."

Now what had she meant by that he wondered as once again fixed his gaze on his size nine feet.

CHAPTER 6

THE THIRD RULE

Nica's booming voice brought Pete back to the situation at hand. "I'm sure you will all agree that we have very few rules here, and the ones we do have are reasonable and important."

Nica's eyes scanned the group as they nodded their agreements. With a satisfied look upon his face Nica turned his gaze upon the brown-haired girl who was standing, "Kaya, please remind us all of our final rule."

Pete's eyes were locked with Kaya's eyes as the girl spoke directly to him. "We must not have contact with any humans at any time."

"Ah, yes, and now, don't you think that this rule is an important one?" Pete felt Nica was also speaking directly to him.

He wanted to ask why it was so important, and before he realized it he was saying, "I don't understand why it's such a big deal. What could it hurt?"

Nica did not like to have his authority questioned, but he did a good job of holding his anger in tact. However, his smile looked forced, his voice was tight, and instead of answering Pete's question he asked, "Is there anyone here who can help Pete out with this?"

No one seemed willing to say anything. He laughed and coaxed in a good-natured manner, "Come now, surely you all remember what you were told about contact with people on the Earth. Who haven't we heard from yet?"

His eyes roved around the group and settled on a round-faced, round-bodied boy with red hair and matching freckles. "Rusty, can you help us out?"

Rusty turned his pudgy face away from Nica to look at Brice who was sitting beside him. Rusty was thirteen and seemed to find life tolerable only by attaching himself to someone stronger. Since landing on the cloud he had become Brice's shadow. Whatever Brice said Rusty agreed with, and wherever Brice went Rusty was usually right beside him.

Pete felt sorry for the boy who was now looking back up at Nica and moving his mouth in an effort to make some sound come out. At last his high, nervous voice managed to say, "I think it has something to do with contamination."

Nica responded, "Ah, yes, thank you, Rusty." But before Nica could utter another word scuffling sounds came from his other side.

All eyes turned toward the sounds.

A girl with wild, brown hair and tattered clothes was beating on Polly with her fists and yelling at her to take it back.

Polly was yelling back that she didn't have to take anything back. She was also trying to push Tess away. Soon, the two girls were rolling all around the ground engaged in the most physical fighting Pete had ever seen between two girls

Everyone watched the scuffle. Some of the kids started yelling at them.

At first, Pete sat and watched the two girls in amazement. Then he glanced up at Nica, who was also watching.

Pete noticed a look of amusement upon their leader's face. He jumped up and dashed over to the fighting girls. He grabbed Tess and pulled her away from Polly. He held on to her even though she was now kicking and hitting at him.

Tess began shouting at Pete to let go. All at once she went limp and collapsed onto the cloud. Pete couldn't hold the sturdy girl up, so he sat on her legs and held her arms behind her back.

Tess's yelling turned to loud wailing.

Nica walked over to them and said, "That will do, Pete. I am sure Tess will sit quietly now." He folded his arms in front of him and continued, "You will sit quietly now, won't you, Tess?" His voice sounded more like a command than a request.

Pete got up off the girl and slipped back to his place beside Billy Fred. There were now several kids standing around Tess who was sitting up and attempting to rub away her tears.

No one spoke. Everyone watched Tess as they waited for a word of explanation.

None came. Tess had put on a pout and refused to look up at any of them. She was staring down at the cloud in front of her as if by ignoring them they would all go away and leave her alone.

Instead of addressing the unhappy girl Nica spoke to Polly, "What is this all about, Polly?"

The girl either did not hear Nica, or she was deliberately giving the impression that she did not hear. She was turned away busily smoothing her hair and dress back into place.

Nica asked a little louder, "Polly?"

She jerked around with a startled expression on her face. "Oh, I'm sorry. What did you want?"

Nica repeated his question, "What is this all about?"

Polly sniffed and drew herself up haughtily. "Tess is crazy. She attacked me for no reason."

Somehow, Pete doubted the truth of her statement.

Tess came out of her pout to yell, "That's a lie! She's mean, and she called me names." She looked as if she were about to attack again.

Nica asked in a gentle voice, "Is that true, Polly?"

Polly swung her long hair as she answered, "Well, what if it is? She smells bad and looks like a bum."

"I do not," Tess shouted and jumped to her feet.

"You do, too," Polly shouted back.

Tess lunged, but Nica caught her. "That will do. Both of you will report to me after we are through here. I believe I can find some way to help you work out your disagreement."

Both girls froze. Tess dropped back down right where she was. Polly made her way over close to where Gene was hunched with his arms around his knees. She sniffed at the boy and settled herself upon the cloud.

Pete looked at Billy Fred who was looking soberly back at him. Then Pete noticed Jo Jo's look of concern.

Immediately, as if sensing his gaze, Jo Jo's mouth turned up into an impish grin, and he chanted, "Sticks and stones may break her bones, but words will never hurt her—unless they're Polly's. Hers are more lethal than a scud missile."

CHAPTER 7

THE SKUNK

Pete was not feeling a bit better—not even after Nica's glowing description of what their lives were going to be like in the future. That is, if everyone would just be patient and follow the few, little rules they had. Then it would be only a matter of time before they would be leaving the cloud and going to a wonderful place where everything would be perfect.

As he often did Pete was sitting off by himself. He wished he could get rid of the growing scepticism in his mind that the wonderful place was a figment of Nica's imagination.

Pete was trying really hard not to lean over the edge of the cloud and look for people on Earth. He probably shouldn't put himself in such a position to be tempted, but here he was, and he was definitely tempted.

"Hi, Pete," a soft voice came from behind him.

Pete whirled around and found himself looking into wide, hazel eyes. The crippled boy, Lennie, was standing there slouched over his crutches. He was an exceptionally thin boy with a thatch of light brown hair flopping down onto his forehead, and despite being able to move without taking steps he was still clinging to his crutches as if his life depended on it.

For the first time this puzzled Pete, and so after his own hello he asked, "Lennie, why do you still use your crutches? You don't need them here, do you?"

Lennie's sad face became even sadder as he answered, "Well, yes, I guess I do. I mean, I can move anywhere I want to without moving my legs, but I don't think I can stand all by myself."

"Have you tried?"

"No, I'm afraid to."

"Why? Seems like it wouldn't hurt to try," Pete persisted.

"Oh," Lennie's voice was tired. "I don't think it would work."

Pete felt his anger rising. Why couldn't the boy try? Pretty stupid to drag around a couple of boards when you might not have to. He started to voice this opinion, but at the look in the boy's eyes he bit his lip and said nothing. Lennie was hurting in ways Pete knew nothing about. Pete knew this with a knowledge from somewhere deep within himself. Again, he did not know how he knew it, but he accepted it as fact.

Pete changed the subject. "Lennie, do you ever lean over and watch the people below?"

The boy answered with little enthusiasm, "Not too often. What's the point?"

"I don't know. Sometimes, I just want to jump right off this cloud and land down there and forget all about this place."

Lennie's face was full of fear. "You wouldn't do it, would you?"

"I guess not," Pete answered, echoing the boy's tired voice.

In a livelier voice Lennie continued, "I mean, you would probably die." His eyes were widened in horror at the thought of such a fate.

"Would I?" Pete asked. "I'm not so sure."

The horror in Lennie's eyes spread to his whole face.

Pete smiled sheepishly. He said, "Ah, Lennie, don't worry. I probably won't take the chance. Forget I said anything. Okay?"

Lennie nodded but didn't look happy.

Pete plopped down on his stomach and hung his head over to do what he had promised himself he would not do—study what was going on below.

He forgot about Lennie as he caught sight of a tiny figure moving along a path winding crookedly through thick trees. He strained his eyes as hard as he could. Suddenly, he was overcome with the knowledge that something was going to happen to this figure jogging along on the country path.

Then just as suddenly he knew that a small, dark object moving through the trees was the cause of the danger.

Pete realized that Lennie was now sitting beside him and also looking at the drama unfolding before their eyes. He said, "Lennie, that person is in danger. I know it."

"Maybe we shouldn't look," Lennie suggested.

"No, it's okay. I'm just interested." Pete tried to play down the urge to do something.

He pointed to the small moving object and asked, "Do you know what that thing is?"

"I can't see it too well. Actually, I'm surprised I can see it at all. We're pretty high up. I'm sure no one down there can see us."

"Yeah, I know. We have better eyesight here than we used to." With a sigh he added, "But I still wish I had better. I'd like to know what it is."

"It's a rabid skunk," a voice above them stated calmly.

"What?" Pete exclaimed as he rolled over to look at the person speaking.

Jo Jo grinned down at him, "Can't you see, Slim? It's black with a stripe running down its back, and it's foaming at the mouth. That makes it a rabid skunk."

"You can see its mouth?" Pete asked in astonishment.

"Sure, can't you?"

"No, I could see something moving, and I guessed it was an animal. But that's all."

Lennie didn't say anything.

Jo Jo leaned over the edge and said, "There's a lady with a red hat and a black jogging suit on, and I think she has Reebok running shoes."

"Cool," Pete breathed out. Cool was his favorite word for anything that pleased or amazed him. Since his arrival here he hadn't used it very often, but now the word had popped out automatically. Jo Jo's eyesight was unbelievable. He teased, "Does she have blue eyes?"

Jo Jo turned and grinned at him, "How did you guess?"

Pete wasn't sure if he was kidding or not. Once again he gazed down at the woman and then at the moving skunk. A sudden rushing of doom enveloped him. He couldn't talk. He didn't think he could move, but then he was moving. He was moving out away from the cloud and then plunging down, down, down.

Pete's aim was good for he found himself very close to the skunk who would be upon the jogger in no time if it didn't veer off into another direction.

Pete tried to think what to do. The skunk was continuing through the trees. It would be on the path at exactly the same time and in exactly the same place as the woman if something didn't stop it. Pete could see fizzing saliva dripping from its mouth.

"Here, hit it with this," a voice spoke from behind him.

A heavy post was shoved into his hands. With no other thoughts and with all his strength Pete moved directly over the sick animal and slammed the post down hard. The skunk fell over and lay still with blood oozing unpleasantly from a gaping hole. Pete looked away from the sickening sight.

From where he was he couldn't see the jogger, so he lifted himself up into the air and looked over the trees. The woman was jogging along as if nothing had happened, and thanks to Pete nothing had happened to her. She hadn't a clue of the danger she had been spared.

"Jo Jo! What are you doing here?" he asked as he lowered himself back down to the ground.

Sadly, Pete realized that he had gotten both himself and Jo Jo into every bit as much danger as the woman jogger had been in before they had rescued her. Possibly even more danger because there was probably no one to help them as they had helped her.

"I'm sorry, Jo Jo. I'm so sorry," he uttered sincerely.

"Don't worry. Be happy." the optimistic boy stated with sparkling eyes before saying, "It isn't over yet. We need to bury this skunk so no predators will eat it and become rabid"

As quickly as they were able the two boys dug into the soft ground with sticks and their hands. They pushed the animal into the shallow grave with the same sticks and covered it with dirt and leaves.

"Let's go," Jo Jo said as he brushed off dirt particles from his hands onto his shorts.

"Go where?" Pete asked in bewilderment.

"Back to the cloud, Silly. We can't stay here. You know that."

Pete looked up into the clouds. There were so many, and he wasn't sure which one was their cloud. He squinted into the brightness and gasped. Was that a tiny, tiny face staring down this way?

"Come on," Jo Jo urged, tugging at him. The two boys raised themselves up into the sky. At an unbelievable speed they zipped up and landed beside Lennie, who was looking even more horrified than he had earlier.

He was not alone!

CHAPTER 8

BRICE CAUSES TROUBLE

"What have you two been up to?" an accusing voice demanded.

Pete stuttered out a reply, "I—we—uh, I—There was a woman who . . ." He broke off and shrugged his shoulders. Then taking a deep breath he confessed, "There was a woman who was in danger of being attacked by a rabid skunk. I didn't mean to, but—but I just had to do something." Both his voice and eyes pleaded for understanding.

"Oh, Pete, how could you?" Kaya's tone changed to exasperation and so did the expression on her face.

She turned to Jo Jo, and now her tone was back to accusing. "And you, Jo Jo, how did you let Pete talk you into such a thing?"

Jo Jo grinned his merry grin, shrugged his own shoulders, and replied, "He didn't," as calmly as if that really was a good explanation for endangering himself.

Vonnie, standing beside Kaya, broke her silence, "Oh, you two. Don't you know you're contaminated now? What are you going to do?" Tears began streaming down her cheeks.

Both Kaya and Lennie looked stricken. Pete's face was stubborn, and Jo Jo's still retained humor, although he certainly didn't have anything to be happy about.

Kaya frowned at the two boys, and Pete knew she was trying to think of a way to help them.

Vonnie said in a tearful voice, "How do you feel? Do you feel contaminated?"

Pete and Jo Jo looked at each other. Pete didn't know about Jo Jo, but he, himself, was feeling only a little tired, sort of like he had played a hard game of baseball. However, now that Vonnie had called his attention to it, he did feel he was breathing a little harder—as if trying to take in more oxygen. He swallowed hard and told himself to quit imagining things.

Pete fixed his eyes upon Kaya sensing that she was the only one who could possibly help them. She was staring off into space. Finally, with her face still turned away from them, she murmured in a quiet, thoughtful voice, "I wish I knew how to run Nica's machine. Then we could give you a treatment. I'm not sure, but it makes sense that it could de-contaminate you."

"I know how to make it work," Lennie declared.

Now everyone's eyes turned to the small figure clutching his crutches and looking at them with an anxious expression upon his thin face.

Kaya's eyes narrowed. She asked, "Are you sure, Lennie. It's very important."

Lennie's face took on an injured look.

"Of course, I'm sure. I've seen Nica do it a lot of time."

"So have I, but I haven't the faintest idea how to make it work. It looks pretty complicated."

"I know I can do it," Lennie insisted. "But I don't know if I should."

Vonnie sniffed and wiped her teary eyes with the back of one hand. She said forcefully, "You have to help Pete and Jo Jo, Lennie."

Looking fearful Lennie said, "I think we should tell Nica. Don't you think he would give them treatments?"

"I'm not so sure," Kaya answered grimly.

Vonnie chimed in, "We can't take the chance."

Lennie asked fearfully, "But what if we get caught?"

"We won't. I'll see to that," Kaya insisted firmly with an expression of determination.

"How?" Pete couldn't help but ask and tried to ignore the strange discomfort starting to spread through his body. He hoped the others did not know how bad he was beginning to feel.

Pete glanced at the oriental boy beside him. Jo Jo's slanted eyes were not quite as mischievous as usual, and it looked like he was breathing harder.

Pete turned his attention back to the tall, brown-eyed girl. Kaya was explaining, "I'll go a little ahead of you—to make sure Nica isn't at the treatment room. If he isn't there I'll wave at you. You know just a casual, friendly wave. If he is there I'll get him to go somewhere with me and keep him away for awhile."

"Okay," Pete said.

Jo Jo asked with uncharacteristic concern, "What if he isn't there, but he comes before we get finished?"

"No problem. As soon as you start the treatments I'll go looking for him. I'll keep him away. I promise." She drew an X across her heart with a finger.

They all headed toward the treatment room. Kaya and Lennie moved quickly ahead of the others.

Pete, Jo Jo, and Vonnie deliberately went a little slower. They didn't want to get there before Kaya checked to make sure Nica was gone.

Before Kaya and Lennie were out of sight Brice surprised them from behind. Rusty was right beside him. They both moved past Pete and Jo Jo without speaking. When Brice reached Vonnie, he said with a sneer, "Hi ya, Blondie. What are ya doing hanging round these losers?"

"Excuse me, Brice, but I really have to go," Vonnie answered.

"Go where?" he demanded. Then twisting his mouth up into an unpleasant smirk he added, "There's not too many places to go on this cloud. How about you come play a game of ping-pong or pool with me?'

"No, I don't want to." Vonnie sounded desperate. Her voice was strained and her eyes troubled as she added with the same note of desperation, "I'm meeting Kaya, and I'm late."

Pete felt he needed to help the girl out, so he stepped up to confront the bully, "Leave Vonnie alone, Brice. Can't you take a hint?"

"Shut up, Bean Pole, and get lost," Brice barked back.

Vonnie lost her troubled look and stated rudely, "You get lost, Brice."

"Oh yeah, well, who's going to make me? I don't think old Bean Pole here and the little twerp beside him can handle it."

Pete grew nervous at the appraising look Brice was giving him. He drew himself up as much as he was able and hoped he looked more fit than he was feeling.

Unexpectedly and with a big grin on his face Jo Jo observed, "Is that Nica coming toward us?"

Brice spun around.

Jo Jo laughed merrily and shouted, "Ha Ha, I gotcha."

"I'll get you for this," Brice threatened as he swung back around.

Vonnie had taken the opportunity Jo Jo's diversion had caused to begin moving away from Brice. However, the bully reacted quickly and grabbed her arm.

Before Pete could think of what to do Billy Fred appeared in front of Brice and Vonnie. He called out gaily, "Hi, gang! Looks like a lot of fun. Can I play?" He grabbed onto Vonnie's free hand and said, "Hey, Vonnie, how can you tell if a blonde . . ."

The girl interrupted in an agitated voice, "Oh, Billy Fred, not now. I'm late meeting Kaya." She twisted and turned in an effort to free herself from both boys' hands.

Billy Fred shrugged, released her hand, and turned to the bigger boy still holding onto the struggling Vonnie and said, "Hey, Brice, since you seem to have some free time on your hands. Uh—at least, you will have as soon as you let go of Vonnie . . ." He wiggled his bushy eyebrows and allowed his voice to trail off suggestively.

At the laughter of the others the bully let go of his grasp on Vonnie.

Billy Fred cut into their laughter to continue, "How about a game of ping-pong? I think Owen is over at the game room, or better yet, maybe Kat and I can take you and your pal here on." He gestured to Rusty and declared, "Ought to be about even." He roared loudly at his insinuation that eight-year-old Kat and he could do better than the two older boys.

Pete breathed a sigh of relief as Brice growled out an acceptance to the challenge and left with Rusty trailing along.

CHAPTER 9

TREATMENTS

The second Brice started off with Billy Fred, Vonnie was off in the direction of the treatment room. The two boys left behind forced themselves to follow her despite the physical desire to collapse onto the softness of the cloud. Pete could not help thinking that now he knew how important the treatments were. Nica had been telling the truth about that.

Pete was moving much more slowly than normal. He felt sluggish, but did manage to keep his body propelling across the surface of the cloud. Vonnie was quickly disappearing ahead of them, and Jo Jo was lagging a little behind Pete.

Pete turned around to check on the smaller boy. He asked quietly, "Are you all right?"

Jo Jo attempted a grin and nodded, "Don't worry. Be happy." But the tone in his voice was muted and did not reflect the message of his words.

When Pete turned back around he saw that Vonnie had stopped and waited. She watched them, and as soon as they were close enough she said, "Come on. Don't you know we need to hurry?"

She looked past Pete and gasped, "Oh, no!" She raced past him and started to grab Jo Jo.

"No! Don't touch him!" Pete exclaimed fearfully.

Vonnie stopped her hand before it reached the sagging boy and exhaled a breath of air, "Oh, do you think if I help him I might become contaminated?"

Pete nodded bleakly, "Go on, Vonnie. See if there's anything you can do to help Lennie get ready for the treatments. We'll make it okay. I know we will."

Tears once again springing into her eyes, the girl nodded with understanding and rushed toward the treatment room.

Pete helped Jo Jo keep going the best he could, and after what seemed like forever, but was really only a few minutes, the two boys reached the entrance to the treatment room. Vonnie was nervously waiting in front of it. Neither Lennie nor Kaya were in sight.

Vonnie whispered, "Lennie's inside. Kaya went to keep Nica away."

Pete nodded and said, "Vonnie, you stay out here and keep guard."

The pretty girl nodded and said, "Okay, but if someone comes what shall I do?"

Wearily Pete answered, "I don't know. Just play it by ear, I guess."

He turned to Jo Jo and said, "You go first. You're smaller. You probably are in more danger."

The smaller boy looked like he was about to argue so Pete reached out and pushed him through the doorway ahead of him.

The treatments were done one at a time in a machine which resembled an old-fashioned telephone booth, except that it was made of some kind of shiny metal. It had no windows, so you couldn't see into it at all.

Lennie turned toward them as they entered. He was seated at a panel of buttons and switches.

"Hurry," he said. "It's ready for one of you."

Pete continued shoving at Jo Jo until the small figure was inside, and the door to the treatment booth was shut.

Pete watched Lennie move switches and poke buttons. It was bewildering to him, but Lennie worked with an air of confidence.

Pete was now gasping for air, and he felt as if he would collapse onto the floor. With every ounce of determination he had he willed himself to relax and breathe calmly and smoothly. He knew he must not panic, but it was very hard not to cry out for help. He propped his weakened body against a wall and waited.

The actual treatment took four minutes, but it felt like four hours to Pete before Lennie quit moving things on the panel and said, "Open the door, Pete, and let Jo Jo out. I'll set up for you."

Although his mind was telling him to move quickly his body refused to obey, but at last Pete's fumbling fingers managed to undo the latch and open the door.

Jo Jo hopped out with his normal grin. His almond-shaped eyes were once again sparkling. "Gee, I feel great. Come on, Pete, get yourself in there."

"Cool," Pete murmured weakly and pushed himself into the booth.

A short while later the three boys stealthily made their way out of the treatment room.

Vonnie looked anxiously at them and then smiled when she realized the two adventurers were back to normal.

The four of them moved as far away from the treatment room as they could get.

Pete was feeling great, but he had learned a lesson. It was dangerous to go to the Earth below. It was really a very stupid thing to do!

CHAPTER 10

WHO ELSE KNOWS?

"Hey, Pete, how's it going?" Billy Fred asked exuberantly.

"Okay," Pete answered cautiously and pretended to stay focused on the video game he was playing in the game room. Pete was not at all sure how to handle any questions the other boy might ask.

"Look, Pete, what's going on?" Billy Fred asked.

"What do you mean?" Pete answered not taking his eyes off his game.

"I mean, yesterday, when I helped you out and got rid of Brice and Rusty for you."

Pete gulped, turned toward Billy Fred and said with genuine gratitude, "Oh, yeah, well, thanks. They're a real pain sometimes." Pete tried to remain cool.

"Sure, any time. Now, tell me. What gives?"

Pete sighed and ran his hand through his curly hair. "I wish I could tell you, Billy Fred, but I just can't."

"Anything to do with your dive over the edge of the cloud?"

Pete stared at the other boy, his mind reeling. If Billy Fred had seen him no telling who else had. He breathed out in a tormented whisper, "You know?"

"Yeah, I saw, but I don't think anyone else did," Billy Fred said.

Pete was relieved. "Are you sure?"

"Pretty sure. I went and checked on the big shots. All three of them were over in Nica's office together. I can't swear about any of the other kids, but I kind of think they were all in the game room since our work time was over."

Pete considered that for a moment before speaking. "Thanks again, Billy Fred. I guess I do owe you an explanation after your rescuing me and all."

The door burst open and Polly sailed into the room screaming, "Help, help, don't let that creature near me."

Tess came flying in right behind her. She grabbed at Polly, but Polly managed to get behind Pete.

Tess dashed after her, but Pete seized Tess's arms and held on tightly. He asked, "Tess, what are you up to now?"

"She's making fun of me. She's always making fun of me."

Polly stepped out from behind Pete. Her pretty features shifted from fear to a calculating look now that Tess was no longer a threat. She smoothed her long, black hair daintily and cooed, "Thank you, Pete. You're my knight in shining armor."

Pete frowned at her and said, "Don't be dumb, Polly, and cut out that mush, or I'll let go of Tess."

Tess used the distraction to pull away from his grip. She lunged at Polly.

Polly squealed like a pig and slid behind Billy Fred, "Oh, save me, save me," she yelled.

Pete tried to recapture Tess, but she slipped from his grasp and grabbed one of Polly's wrists. Tess pulled Polly out from behind Billy Fred, pushed her to the ground, and sat on her.

Polly screamed loudly.

In a voice uncannily like Nica's, Billy Fred said, "Girls, what is the meaning of this?"

Both girls froze. Pete pulled Tess up and held on to her tightly. He said as forcefully as he could, "Get out of here, Polly."

"But I want to play a video game," she complained.

"Do it later. Now leave before I let go of her." This was no idle threat since Tess was wiggling so fiercely he might not have any choice but to let her go."

Oh, all right, but I won't take back what I said. I won't." With that Polly stuck her nose up in the air and left.

Pete held on to the girl who was twisting and turning for all she was worth, but he knew he couldn't hold on to her much longer. In between pants Pete asked, "Tess, how come you let that snob get to you? Can't you just ignore her?"

"No, I can't, and I won't, and sometime I'm going to hurt her bad."

Billy Fred tried, "Now, Tess, why do you want to go and do a thing like that? It would only get you in trouble."

"I don't care. I hate her." Her voice was harsh with emotion.

Pete sighed. How can anyone really hate someone else he wondered. People were just people. His mom had always insisted that there was good in everybody. He had always believed that, too. That is, until now. Was there good in Jez-beel, who had tricked him into coming to this place?

His thoughts were jerked back to the struggling girl when she stomped hard on his left foot.

"Ouch!" he yelled and let go of her.

Tess went flying out the door like a Kansas tornado. Pete and Billy Fred were left alone.

Billy Fred expelled a noisy breath of air and commented, "Wow, what a whirlwind! I'm glad I'm not Polly."

"Don't you think she was just letting off steam? I don't think she'd really hurt Polly."

"I hope you're right. Now, Pal, I haven't forgotten about that explanation you said you owed me."

Pete dropped down onto the floor. "Okay, here goes."

He related the details of his trip to Earth as quickly as he could. Some of the other kids might show up at any time. When he finished he waited for Billy Fred's condemnation of his stupid actions.

What a surprise when all the other boy said was, "Yeah, I understand."

"You do?" Pete exclaimed.

Billy Fred's expression was as serious as his words, "Yeah, Pete. I just wish I'd been with you. I get mighty tired of spending all my time playing games and thinking up jokes, but when you're bored you have to do something."

Pete gazed at him in wonder. Now, who would have thought it? Billy Fred was not all jokes and fun.

CHAPTER 11

PETE'S IDEA

Pete obeyed the rules, but he was even more miserable than ever. Days passed, but he kept reliving how weak he had been after his trip to Earth.

One day, while he was alone in the game room, he forced himself to examine the whole experience. He had really been weak. Not as weak as Jo Jo, though. Was it because Jo Jo was smaller or, maybe, because he was oriental?

A strange idea popped into his mind. Had Nica picked. . . .

"Hello, Pete," Kaya interrupted his thinking as she came into the game room. "What's the weird look on your face all about?"

Pete pulled his thoughts together and said seriously, "Kaya, you'll never believe what I've been thinking about?"

"You're not thinking of making another trip, are you?" the girl asked in a troubled voice.

"No, I've been thinking about how different Jo Jo and I are."

With a quizzical look Kaya said, "So?"

"Yeah, you see . . ."

He was interrupted again. Vonnie swept into the room holding her hands over her ears. When she reached them she cried out dramatically, "Don't let him tell me any more blonde jokes. I can't take any more."

Billy Fred was right behind her, laughing loudly. He stopped his noisy chuckling to ask, "Hey Vonnie, how do you make a blonde's eyes sparkle?"

As usual he didn't wait for an answer but shouted out

triumphantly, "Shine a flashlight in her ear." He exploded into loud laughter. His face was flushed with humor and tears of laughter squeezed out from beneath his droopy eyelids.

Vonnie groaned and pushed her hands harder against her ears. She yelled, "It's not my fault I'm blonde. Blame my parents."

Pete interrupted this time, "See what I mean, Kaya? Vonnie's really different from you. Then not giving the girl time to answer he asked, "What nationality are you?"

"I'm American."

"I know that. We all are, but you have dark eyes, but you're not black like me."

"Gosh, I don't know. I think my ancestors have been American for years, and they probably came from all sorts of places."

Pete looked thoughtful as he turned to Billy Fred. "What about you, Billy?" he asked, noting the boy's short sandy hair, fair skin, and pale blue eyes.

"You mean, like Scottish, and a little English, and a smidgen of Irish, not to mention a French grandmother and an Indian grand something or other."

Pete nodded excitedly and continued, "Yeah, don't you see? Don't any of you see? We're all different."

Kaya looked at him as if he had lost his mind. "Yes, we're all different, but what's the point?"

"Well, I've been wondering. I mean, why we're not all black or all oriental or all mixed up like Billy Fred."

"Oh, I get it. You're wondering if there's some hidden reason behind why Nica got us all up here," Kaya stated.

Before Pete could continue explaining, Brice and Rusty burst into the game room. "Well, if it ain't the black bean pole and the dumb blonde," he said with a sneer, ignoring both Kaya and Billy Fred.

Pete answered in the same mocking tone as Brice had used, "And if it isn't the local bully and his mute henchman."

Rusty blushed furiously.

Brice made a fist and shook it in Pete's face. "You wouldn't say that if you didn't have your female bodyguard with you," he said nastily as he pointed his head toward Kaya.

In a quiet but forceful voice Kaya said, "Brice, won't you ever learn? We aren't ruled by might up here. You'd get along a lot better if you remembered that."

Brice rolled his eyes with contempt. "You think just because everybody lets you talk you know it all, but you don't. You don't know nothin'."

Kaya responded grimly, "Maybe not, but it's still a lot more than you know."

She turned to the others. She said, "Come on, let's go somewhere else to talk."

They trooped out of the game room which was located in the center of the cloud. Places for taking their treatments and making the cloud material, as well as Nica's office and the rooms for sleeping, were clustered close together on one side of the cloud.

Pete and the others headed for the other side of the cloud which had only two shelters. Both of these shelters were very large and were covered twice a day with some of the thick, white material used to disguise the place. The largest building hid the big, bubble-like contraption which had brought them here, and the other was a mysterious, locked building which no one ever seemed to enter.

Much to their surprise they found Jo Jo slumped against the side of the locked building.

"Hi, Jo Jo, come on with us. We need to talk," Pete invited.

They found a spot in front of the shelter, and the five of them settled down into a circle so they could see anyone approaching from any direction.

"Okay, Pete, now what's this all about?" Kaya demanded.

Suddenly Pete was feeling a little silly about this ideas. He swallowed and said, "It might not be anything, but I got to thinking about all of us being different, and I had an idea that maybe it was deliberate. You know what I mean?"

Kaya answered, "Well, you're right about us being different. I know Kat is Hispanic, and Gene is Cherokee."

"How do you know that? I mean, that Gene is Cherokee and not from some other Native American tribe."

"He told me," Kaya answered.

"He did? I didn't think he ever spoke to anyone."

"He doesn't say much, that's for sure. But we were working together one day, and I wanted to know so I asked him," Kaya explained.

"Cool," Pete responded with admiration.

Kaya looked embarrassed and said, "Now, where were we?"

Vonnie prompted, "You just told us that Gene is Cherokee."

"Tess must be Irish," Pete said thoughtfully. "She certainly has the old Irish temper."

"Pretty Polly is probably partly black and partly white, don't you think?" asked Billy Fred.

"Yeah," Pete agreed. "Owen's pretty much a mixture, too, I think. He looks like a typical white American. I'm not sure about either Rusty or Brice. What do you all think?"

"I think Brice is from another planet, and poor old Rusty is a zombie," Billy Fred answered and pulled his face into a grotesque shape.

Vonnie giggled, "For once, Billy Fred, I agree with you."

"Come on, Guys. Pete is serious," Kaya scolded.

"Okay," Billy Fred sobered. "So, Pete, even if you're right, why did Nica bring us here?" His face now showed nothing but interest.

"Yeah, Pete, and why do you think different types of kids were brought here? What gave you such an idea?" Kaya asked as she pushed her straight, brown hair away from her face. Her eyes caught his own and seemed to insist on a logical answer.

Pete did his best, "Well, you see, I didn't choose to come. Jez-beel tricked me."

Jo Jo spoke up, "I'm not surprised. I don't think that lady does anything on the up and up."

"Why do you say that, Jo Jo?" asked Kaya.

"She tricked me, too."

Kaya drew her lips into a round, silent O. She looked around at the others. "Were any of the rest of you tricked?" she asked quietly.

Vonnie answered first, "No, I wanted to come. I was miserable. I would have done anything to get away from my family." She shuddered and added in a sad voice, "I was abused. Leaving there was like a dream come true."

Vonnie's lovely face reflected the horror she was remembering, and Pete wished he knew something to say to wipe away the horror. However, he didn't, so he turned his sympathetic eyes away and rested them on Kaya.

Kaya was saying, "I wasn't tricked either. I didn't ever have a father that I know of, and my mother drank all the time and had smelly, ugly boyfriends. I had awful clothes like this, and the kids at school made fun of me."

For the first time Pete realized that Kaya's ragged jeans and wrinkled, faded blouse weren't all that attractive. Funny, he hadn't even noticed her clothes before. Not that it was too important up here. Everyone always wore the same thing. They were superhuman now and didn't have to worry about ordinary things like clothes and eating and cleaning and brushing teeth. They only had to worry about getting their treatments.

Pete turned to Billy Fred who was agreeing with Kaya. "Yeah, I wanted to come, too. A place with everything I ever wanted. It sounded great! Much better than moving from one foster home to another—and another—and another."

Sadly Vonnie asked, "Do you think there's not really a wonderful place like Nica keeps telling us about? That he has no intention of ever getting us off this cloud?"

Kaya answered for all of them, "We don't know, Vonnie."

Everyone was quiet, each trying to make some sort of sense out of their situation. Kaya was the first to speak, "Okay, Pete, why do you think you were tricked?"

"The only reason I can think of is because Jez-beel needed to bring a black kid, and time was running out. We took off in that bubble thing right after I got in it. I didn't have a chance to get out."

They were all silent. Then, as if by magic, Sadju was standing behind Jo Jo and smiling at them with his ugly, oily smile which didn't seem like a real smile at all.

CHAPTER 12

KAT

"Here you are," Sadju announced as if it were the greatest discovery ever made. "You were missed."

"Oh?" Kaya questioned. "Why? Our work is all done. This is free time, isn't it?"

"Of course, but we wanted to make sure you were safe." He bent at the waist toward Kaya and grimaced—not a real look of concern in Pete's eyes. It was more like how the wolf must have looked at Little Red Riding Hood.

"Why wouldn't we be safe?" Pete demanded.

Vonnie gasped aloud at Pete's boldness and quickly slapped her hand over her mouth.

The others remained quietly attentive.

Sadju rubbed his hands together, looked pleased about something, and replied, "Although there are not many, Pete. There are a few dangers."

Pete kept himself from shivering. There was something very menacing about this strange-looking man.

A loud, shrill whistle erupted all around them.

Sadju ordered, "Quick, everyone into the shelter." He pointed to the building which housed the bubble-like vehicle.

They scampered wildly toward it.

Billy Fred slid the large door open. He made a sweeping gesture with his arms for the others to enter ahead of him.

Pete held back and was sorely tempted to make a dash away from the doorway. He had an urge to stand up on top of the shelter and wave his arms.

As if sensing his rebellion Sadju placed a hand on Pete's shoulder, squeezed it, and said in a nasty-nice voice, "It would be unwise if any of us were seen, Pete. I guarantee it."

Pete slid out from under the unpleasant man's hand and walked swiftly into the shelter.

Sadju waited for Billy Fred to follow Pete. Then, he slipped inside and pulled the door into place.

The whistling continued, though now its shrillness was muffled by the walls of the building.

Pete asked nonchalantly, "Sadju, why didn't we go into that other shelter? We were much closer to it."

Sadju's expression closed, and Pete had no idea what the man was thinking. His answer was vague, and Pete was sure the man was not giving an honest answer.

Sadju said, "You will see one of these days, Pete. For now, it does not hold anything of interest to you, but one day soon you will see."

Pete shivered at the man's tone. Perhaps, he didn't ever want to know what the building held.

They did not have to stay hidden in the shelter for long. By the time Sadju had answered Pete's question the whistling had ceased and all was quiet.

The warning whistle had gone off only a few times before. Nica usually kept their cloud far away from places where aircraft would be close enough to detect their presence. He said it would be dangerous for anyone to look down and see them moving effortlessly around on a cloud. In the rare cases where there was a threat, some kind of device—radar or something more sophisticated—warned them of aircraft too close for comfort. Then they were all to get into one of the shelters. It didn't matter which one. All the buildings were covered daily with the cloud material to keep them camouflaged.

Pete had often wondered how this place could exist without being detected by the radar used by people on the Earth. Maybe, one of these days he would ask Nica. It might be interesting to see what the man said.

Sadju opened the door, and they all trooped out.

As they were sliding the door back into place Nica and the little, Hispanic girl came up to them. Kat was looking quite pleased with herself. Pete could tell the girl was up to something.

However, Nica smiled pleasantly at them and said, "Ah, I see you are all safe."

There was that word *safe* again. Pete asked irritably, "Were you really worried about us?"

"Of course, Pete. I want all my kids to be safe—safe and happy." He smiled directly at Pete and asked, "Are you happy, Pete?"

Not really understanding why Nica would ask that question Pete answered cautiously, "I guess so, but I get kind of restless."

"I would have thought there would be more than enough competitions in the game room, and also outside. I am sure you have plenty of game equipment."

As Pete murmured an agreement Nica put his arm around his shoulders and said soothingly, "Besides, it will not be long before we go to that place I've told you about. Be patient a little while longer."

Pete edged away from the unwanted arm on his shoulders and tried to read Nica's eyes. Was the man telling them the truth?

Kat said, "See, Nica, I told you they were all together here, didn't I?"

"Yes, Little One, you did, and I appreciate your concern for the others." His smile was now directed toward the cute, black-haired girl.

She dimpled happily. "I heard them talking."

Pete held his breath.

Kaya showed her quick thinking. She laughed and said gaily, "Oh, Kat, were you listening to our jokes?"

Nica raised his eyebrows quizzically and said, "You were joking?"

"Yes, Billy Fred loves jokes, and we were all trying to top him with our own jokes."

"Oh, and did you?" the man pressed.

"Hun?" Kaya asked dumbly.

"Did you top him with your jokes?"

Kaya laughed again, "No way! Billy Fred's the expert."

Kat looked mutinous as if she wanted to deny Kaya's words. The little girl tugged on Nica's arm.

"Yes, Kat. What is it?"

"I didn't hear anything funny."

Disaster! Had Kat been close by listening, and they hadn't seen her? Quickly, Pete spoke up, "Gosh, Kat, were you hiding? We didn't see you."

She replied scornfully, "Of course, you didn't see me."

Not wanting to give the eight-year-old time to repeat anything she might have overheard Pete said, "How come you didn't come join us, Kat?"

Billy Fred added, "Yeah, we had some great jokes. Mine were the best, of course."

He stood tall and stiff with his hand over his heart.

Kat replied angrily, "I didn't think you wanted me. No one wants me."

Nica patted the little girl on the head and assured her, "Kat, that was in your old life, back down there on Earth. Things are different here. I am sure all of them would have wanted you."

Kat looked confused.

Pete held his breath again and didn't take his eyes off the girl.

Kat allowed her large, black eyes to rove all around the group of kids.

Vonnie smiled sweetly at her, and Pete patted her clumsily on the shoulder.

Billy Fred was serious for a change. He said, "Of course, we want you around, Kat."

Jo Jo grinned and said, "The more the merrier!"

Nica's smile was beginning to droop. He said, "I need to get back and check on the course of our vehicle."

"Don't you have time to listen to Billy Fred's best joke?" Kaya asked innocently.

"I only wish I could. Maybe some other time, eh, Billy?"

"Any time, Nica, any time. I got a million of them."

"Come on, Sadju, we had better check on some things."

The two men disappeared.

"Just like Aladdin's genie," Jo Jo observed.

They all agreed.

Since arriving on the cloud all the kids had learned to move very fast through the air, though none of them could transport themselves like the three adults. They appeared and disappeared as if by magic.

Pete wondered if some day, when he had been here long enough, he would be able to come and go as fast as lightning. Hmmmmm, that was something to work at. Maybe, he could learn to do it if he really worked at it.

This interesting idea was interrupted by Kat's whining voice as she demanded, "Did you mean it?"

In a startled voice Kaya answered, "What are you talking about, Kat?"

"Did you really mean you like to have me around?"

Pete noticed Kaya cross her fingers behind her back as she said cheerfully, "Of course, Kat. I'm sorry you didn't know that. We all had bad times on Earth just like you, so here we have to stick together."

Kat's face lit up.

Pete was ashamed of himself. He had been so busy feeling sorry for himself, he hadn't even worried about any of the other kids. Well, he would change that. Instead of wasting his time worrying about helping people on Earth, he would try to help the other kids up here, and he would start with Kat. She was about the size of his sister, Joni. An overwhelming wave of homesickness swept over him, and he had to fight the moisture threatening to erupt in his eyes.

Kaya was still talking. Pete forced himself to tune back into her voice just in time to hear her say with a trace of conspiracy in her voice, "Kat, how did you happen to know we were over here?"

"I heard you," she answered with a scornful look.

"Yes, I know that's what you told Nica, but how did you get close enough to hear us without us seeing you?"

"Oh, I don't have to get close."

"I don't understand," the older girl stated in a puzzled voice.

Kat said, "I didn't have to be close. I saw you heading this way a while ago, so I just started listening."

"Where were you?" Pete burst in with his own question.

"Over in the dorm reading a book. I looked out the window and saw you all walking this way."

"You heard us from clear over there?" Billy Fred exclaimed.

"Of course," Kat replied calmly.

"A real little pitcher with big ears," Jo Jo said with a chuckle.

"You heard everything we said?" Kaya probed.

"Yeah, and you weren't telling jokes," Kat said, her voice full of suspicion. "You told Nica you were telling jokes, but you weren't."

"Oh, my gosh!" Pete exclaimed. He was thinking. The worse tattle-tale he had ever known in his life, and she had overheard every word they had said.

CHAPTER 13

TEMPTATION

Kat had just dropped a bombshell. She claimed she had overhead everything Pete and the others had said. Could she have already told Nica some of the things they had discussed?

While Pete's mind was running away with all kinds of thoughts, Kaya had taken charge. She was asking, "Kat, did you tell Nica what we were saying?"

"No, but I'm going to," Kat spat out.

"Why?" Kaya asked.

Momentarily caught off guard, Kat stared silently up at the older girl for several seconds before answering rudely, "I am, that's all."

"Kat, it would just make Nica mad. You wouldn't want him to be mad, would you?" Kaya continued her attack.

Kat frowned, but then brightened. "He'd be mad at you guys—not me."

"How do you know he wouldn't be mad at you, too, especially since you didn't tell him at first? Why, I bet he would think you were making it all up just to get attention."

"I don't care. I'm going to tell him."

Pete had an idea. "Kat, did you know I had a little sister just about your age?"

Kat turned her black eyes upon him and said, "Really? I wish I'd had one. Then, maybe, I wouldn't have had to leave Mama and come here."

"Why did you come?"

She answered fiercely, "My mama didn't love me. She only loved my brothers. They got to do anything they wanted. If they were naughty, she didn't care. She'd just say, 'Kat, tattling isn't nice. You must not tattle on your bothers all the time.' I wanted to make her sad."

Anger exploded into Pete's mind. How dare Nica convince this little girl to leave a mother who was probably frantic about her only daughter's disappearance.

Pete controlled his anger and said quietly, "Oh, Kat, I'm sorry. I really am. I know you must miss your family an awful lot. I do, too. Do you think you might play a game with me sometime or read to me like Joni used to? It would help me a lot."

It must have been the right approach, for Kat's look brightened. "Really, Pete. Do you really mean it?"

"Of course, I do. In fact, let's go play your favorite video game right now."

"Really?" she exclaimed again.

After a hasty good-bye to the others, Pete and Kat headed off toward the game room. Kat was happily chattering, but Pete was only half listening. His mind was busy wondering about Kat's incredible hearing.

As soon as Kat paused in her flow of words Pete asked, "Kat, can you hear what Nica says when he's in his office?"

"Oh no," the little girl answered in a bubbly voice.

Matching her tone Pete pressed for more information. "You mean, you've tried but couldn't, or you just haven't ever tried?"

Suspicion entered Kat's voice as she shot back a question of her own, "Why do you want to know?"

Pete grinned encouragingly, "Oh, sometimes I'm just curious. You know, like you were when you listened to us. Except I'm not lucky enough to have the hearing you do."

Kat grinned back, "Yeah, I guess it is lucky. Kind of weird, though."

Pete agreed, "Yes, a lot of things up here are weird."

Kat nodded and said, "I tried to listen once when I saw Jez-beel and Nica go into his office, but I didn't hear them."

"Would you try again, Kat. I mean right now?"

"I thought you wanted to play a video game with me." Her face scrunched up into a pout, and her voice hardened.

Pete backed off. He didn't want to make Kat mad. He grinned down at her and challenged, "Which game do you think you can beat me at?"

* * * * *

Sometime later after playing video games with Kat and working with Sadju producing cloud material, Pete made his way over to his favorite place to be alone. It was close to the edge of the cloud, but he was not planning to watch things down on Earth. He just wanted a quiet place to sort things out in his mind.

Confusing thoughts were coursing through his brain. He believed Nica was up to no good, but he couldn't prove it, or for that matter do anything about it. He was dependent on the man for life.

Pete shuddered and thought. This must be how the slaves had felt. Helpless, hopeless, utterly dependent on their owners for life. Chills ran up and down his spine. He wouldn't become a slave to anyone. *He wouldn't!*

Defiantly he leaned over and gazed at the Earth. It was a clear day, and he could see the tops of lots of trees. The cloud moved calmly over the trees, and now Pete could see fields. He watched until the fields met the outskirts of a small town. Nica usually steered clear of towns, but then this one didn't look like much of one.

When the cloud had moved directly over the town, Pete strained his eyes to make out what was going on below. There were cars moving along the streets, and some kids were playing in yards.

He caught sight of a kid on a bicycle. Pete smiled as he watched the tiny figure moving down the street. He had never owned a bike. He had ridden one a few times when friends were feeling generous. It would have been great to zip along like this kid was doing.

Pete tensed. A large semi-truck was speeding into town on what must be a highway. A familiar sense of doom hit him, and Pete knew the kid would be in the path of the truck in seconds. Could he make it down there in time to keep the truck from hitting the kid? Without considering the consequences he started off the cloud.

"I wouldn't do that," a low, silky voice spoke from above him. "Nica would not like it."

Pete jerked around to stare into Jez-beel's strange, green eyes. "But that truck is going to hit that kid on the bike," he explained.

At the amused look in Jez-beel's eyes Pete realized it was already too late. He looked back down to see the truck stopped, a figure lying in the street, and people quickly gathering.

He shouted angrily as he pulled himself back from his position of half on and half off the cloud, "I could have saved him. I know I could have."

"But at what price, Pete?" Jez-beel asked in a calm voice, her face smooth and beautiful as if the tragedy below hadn't touched her at all.

"I don't care about the price."

"Don't you?" Her eyes narrowed, and the green slivers peeking out seemed to command him to listen. She said in a low, menacing tone, "Have you ever gasped for breath hoping for just one more? Have you ever felt so weak you weren't sure you could move your body even one little inch?"

Her words hit home. Pete did know how it felt. Dread spread in his brain as he remembered how awful he had felt as he waited outside the treatment booth. He had been very near death—very near never having another breath, never moving his body another inch.

Pete wanted to shout out that he didn't care, but he couldn't because he did care. He did want to stay alive, even if alive meant a very weird life in this crazy place.

Jez-beel seemed to know she had convinced him. She smiled with a half smile on her lips and an unnerving gleam in her eyes, "Come on, Pete. Let's move away from the edge. You know, you should not let yourself get involved in the old world. You are new and in a new world. Enjoy it. Come on, let's go somewhere else, and we will talk."

She rested her hand on his arm.

A violent response welled up inside Pete. He shook off her hand and said bluntly, "You tricked me into coming here. I didn't want to, but you tricked me. How come?"

"Now, Pete, you know that is not true. You hated that place where you lived. Don't you remember?" Jez-beel asked in a cunning tone.

"I hated the apartment, but I didn't hate my family, and I never would have left them, and you know it."

Jez-beel's beautiful face twisted into a sneer, but her voice was controlled and as smooth as silk as she said, "Pete, take this advice. Don't ever let Nica know, or you may be extremely sorry. Also, stay away from the edge of the cloud. There is nothing for you down there on Earth any more—nothing at all."

"If that's a threat . . ." Pete started but stopped in mid-sentence for Jez-beel had disappeared.

CHAPTER 14

REBELLION

"I don't know how much longer I can stand it here," Pete declared. "It's like being in prison."

He was sitting with his back against an outside wall of the boy's dormitory. Kaya, Vonnie, Billy Fred, and Jo Jo were with him. They had finished their last work detail for the day, and it was not yet dark. They had gathered in the game room and decided to move to this spot to talk because they could keep an eye on Nica's office without being too obvious about it. Also, it was far enough away, so they couldn't be overheard. That is, unless their leader had hearing as remarkable as Kat's.

"I don't know about that, but I guess I'm getting a little tired of playing games," Kaya agreed.

"Don't let Nica hear you say that. He'll probably double your work time. How would you like that?" Jo Jo quipped.

"Nah, he wouldn't do that. He would probably not let us work at all, and then we would have to play games twenty-four hours a day," Pete shot back, his good humor surfacing.

Before their laughter had died down Billy Fred said in an overly loud voice, "Hey, Vonnie, you ever hear about the blonde who did nothing but play games all day?"

"No, and I'm sure I don't want to," Vonnie managed to get out before Billy Fred jumped to the punch line.

With a sulky expression Billy Fred retaliated, "Okay, then, I'm never going to tell you. You can beg. You can plead."

Vonnie rolled her eyes heavenward.

Without pausing, the jokester turned his attention to the other girl, "Kaya, I'm sure you have a better sense of humor than Vonnie. See if you can solve this riddle?"

Kaya shrugged but remained silent.

Billy Fred continued with a flourish, "What's black and blue and brown?"

Kaya, too, answered quickly before Billy Fred could supply the punch line. She said, "Oh, I don't know. How about scrambled eyes?"

"Yuk! Kaya, That's gross." Vonnie made a face.

The others laughed even louder than before, except for Billy Fred.

"Hey, Kaya, I'm the joke teller," he scolded and pulled his face into basset hound sadness.

Laughingly, Kaya said, "Okay. I'll try to remember that. Now, tell me the right answer, so we can get on to more important things."

"A brunette who told too many blonde jokes," he answered, but didn't roar with his usual loud laughter. Somehow, his joke wasn't so funny after Kaya's scrambled eyes answer.

He turned to Pete and said, "I think I know what you mean, though. Goofing off all the time does get a little old. Why, I think I'd even enjoy a little, old math assignment.

"Not me," Vonnie cut in, "But I do wish I had something to do that took some thinking."

Kaya said, "Maybe, we could come up with some kind of school for ourselves."

"Cool," Pete responded, "Any ideas about how to do it?"

"No, but I'll think about it," Kaya replied with a thoughtful look.

Pete nodded, then changed the subject, "You know, Guys, I think what we really need to do is to try and find out what Nica really has in mind. I can't believe he's just a nice guy helping out a few unhappy kids. Can you?"

Four pairs of troubled eyes stared at Pete.

Jo Jo was the first to speak. "No, Nica isn't in this for charity, but nothing else makes sense."

"Nothing much makes sense any more," Kaya said. "Now that Pete has started me thinking about it I find it hard to believe we all actually agreed to go with such strange creatures. Do you think they cast a spell on us?"

"You mean like witches?" Vonnie asked nervously.

"Toil and trouble on the double. Make these kids come in my bubble." Jo Jo chanted.

Billy Fred held his nose and said in a nasal voice, "That stinks."

Jo Jo shrugged and grinned, "You could do better?"

Kaya stated in a firm tone, "Don't even try, Billy Fred. We need to get back on track. We really have to find out more about this place and Nica. I think if we organize we can learn a lot."

Vonnie sat up on her knees and leaned toward the others. She said in a subdued voice, "We'll have to be careful. Those three pop up here and there all the time. They might even be listening to us right now."

"That's a chance we'll have to take if we're going to do anything at all. Otherwise, we might as well give up and play games day in and day out." Kaya said.

Billy Fred interjected tartly, "Should be no problem spying on them. Sounds easy to me."

"Billy Fred, be serious for once," Kaya retorted.

"I am serious—for once—as you so flatteringly put it. But you sound so matter of fact about it, and I don't know how we can possibly pull it off."

"Yes," Vonnie agreed as she dropped back into a sitting position. "Even if we do manage to find out anything, what good will it do us?" she asked.

Pete's temper flared, and he spoke much more loudly than he should have, "What do you want to do then? Nothing? Well, I won't sit around doing nothing. I'm not going to be a slave for those three without a fight."

Realizing he was too loud he dropped his voice and declared fervently, "I'd rather die."

Reactions of the others were varied. Jo Jo and Billy Fred both looked as if they understood his outburst, and Kaya's expression was one of concern.

Tears sprang up in Vonnie's eyes as she pleaded, "Oh, Pete, don't say such a thing. Please, don't ever say such a thing."

Pete calmed down and tried to assure the sensitive girl, "Vonnie, I won't do anything foolish. I was just letting off steam. I don't really want to die, but no matter what the rest of you decide, I've got to do something. I just don't know what."

"Well, I do," Kaya stated firmly. "I mean, I know how to start."

"How?" the others chorused.

Kaya explained, "We have to organize. Just like I told you. We take turns watching and observing the three of them instead of playing games all the time. Then we get together and compare things."

"What good will that do?" asked Vonnie.

"I'm not really sure, but at least it gets us started, and we just might learn something to help us know what to do next."

Pete nodded, "I agree. Right now we don't have anything to go on."

"I know the more people we get involved the chancier it would be, but Lennie saved Pete and me. I think we ought to let him know what's going on," Jo Jo said with more force than usual.

Running his hand through his sandy hair Billy Fred disagreed firmly, "I know he's a good guy, but I don't think we ought to let anyone else know."

"Yes, and we've all got to agree to not say anything to anyone else no matter what," Kaya stated. Then she added in a scornful voice and with a disgusted look. "We certainly wouldn't want our adult role models to become suspicious."

Vonnie shuddered, "I wouldn't want that awful Sadju to find out anything. He scares me."

"Yes," Pete agreed, "or Jez-beel either. I wouldn't put anything past her."

With a serious look on her face Kaya added, "Or, for sure, Nica. He's not as nice as he tries to make us all think."

Jo Jo chimed in, "I'll second that. He runs the whole thing, you know. What he says goes."

"Kind of scary, isn't it? Now, let's get back to our planning,"

Kaya said. "We need to divide up our free time, so that each of us knows when to be spying on Nica."

"Don't you think we all should be alert all the time?" Pete asked, "I mean, try to learn everything we can."

Kaya responded, "Of course, but we also need to be organized, so that we aren't all trying to spy on Nica at the same time. It would be a little ridiculous for all of us to start turning up too often, don't you think?"

"I sure wish one of us had Kat's ability to hear things without being anywhere in the vicinity. That could really come in handy," Pete voiced his new thought.

"Yeah, but we wouldn't dare let her in on our plan. She'd have it blabbed all over the place in no time," Billy Fred commented.

Pete sighed, "You're right. She does like to tattle, but she's a pretty good kid."

Vonnie's eyes teared up, "I really like Kat, but it's better if we don't tell her even if she could help a lot."

"We'll just have to do the best we can with our own meager abilities," Kaya stated firmly.

"Me thinks our meeting is over. Here comes the elephant-eared monster now," Jo Jo announced dramatically.

Pete popped up and started toward Kat whose dark, wavy locks were blowing back from her face as she rushed toward them. Pete swallowed his hello when he saw that Kat's face was full of fury.

"I heard you," she declared with just as much anger in her voice as was shooting from her black eyes. "I heard what you said."

The others all groaned, except for Vonnie. Her eyes were brimming with the inevitable tears which seemed to flow so easily from her eyes.

"Don't worry. Be happy," was Jo Jo's predictable contribution.

CHAPTER 15

OVER THE EDGE AGAIN

"Do you think Kat will keep her promise not to tell anyone else about what we're doing?" Billy Fred asked Pete.

The two were lounging in Pete's favorite spot at the edge of the cloud.

Pete considered the idea carefully before answering, "I think she means to, but I don't know if she can. She talks so much she could say something and not even realize it."

Billy Fred nodded, "She's sure one fast talker. You know, I can hardly get in a word with her around. Hard to believe, isn't it?" he asked with a grin. He knew he had a reputation of a talker.

True to form he continued before Pete could have possibly spoken, "I know Kaya thinks if we all take turns being with her she won't have an opportunity to blab, but I'm not so sure it'll work."

This time he paused and let Pete respond.

"It might work," Pete said in a hopeful voice as he began plunging his hand in and out of the soft cloud material. "And she certainly can make our job easier. She just has to tune in at the right time, and she can hear all kinds of things."

"Amazing," Billy Fred commented. "I wonder if anybody else can do it. What if old Brice the Bully or his devoted companion, Rusty, can hear that well? Or Pretty Polly?" The boy pulled his face into a grotesquely horrified expression with both eyes crossed and his mouth hanging open.

Pete laughed at the other boy's comical face, but quickly sobered, "If any of those three can hear like Kat does, we might as well forget the whole thing."

Billy Fred's face was back to normal. "Well, anyway, Kat is a whole lot easier to be with than some of the other characters in this place."

"That's for sure. I just had a heck of a time with Tess and Gene a while ago. One's a terror in motion, and the other's as quiet as a mouse. But I reckon it does make sense for us not to spend too much time with just us. We don't want Nica or the others to get suspicious about the times we do get together."

"I wonder if we will ever learn anything helpful," Billy Fred said gloomily.

"Sure, we will. It's just a matter of time, especially with Kat helping." Pete wasn't as confident as he tried to sound.

Almost mechanically, with no conscious thought, Pete flipped himself over onto his stomach and gazed down at the scene below. He said slowly, "Billy Fred, do you ever watch what goes on down there?"

"Sometimes, but not like you do. You get so involved in what's happening. It's more like watching TV for me. Kind of like it's not real things going on down there."

Pete answered but did not take his eyes off the scene below, "I've been trying not to watch, but I just can't help it."

He began examining more closely the activity below. They were over a rural area as they usually were. A small figure caught Pete's attention. He watched, trying to decide what the child was doing, for it had to be a child. It was so tiny.

"Billy Fred, look. Can you make out what that tiny figure is, and what it's doing?" He pointed to the figure.

"Afraid not," was the other boy's unhelpful answer.

It didn't matter what Billy Fred said, anyway. That same old sense of doom had already invaded Pete's mind. Something awful was going to happen. The child below was in danger.

Anxiously he searched for signs of another person. He spotted a group of people some distance away. He looked back at the child. He noticed that the child was beside a pool of water. Could the people below see the child at the water's edge?

"Oh no," Pete moaned. The child had fallen and was now submerged in the water.

With no thought or hesitation Pete plunged over the side, and before he even realized what he was doing he was at the edge of the pond. He dove into the water and quickly located the child, a small girl. He pulled her out and placed her on her stomach. He turned her head to one side and checked her throat with his finger. He began gently using the artificial respiration techniques he had learned at the Boy's Club.

Immediately, the girl began choking. Muddy water spouted from her mouth. She coughed uncontrollably for a few seconds and then began to whimper.

Pete picked her up in his arms and began soothing her, "It's okay. You're all right, Little Girl. You'll be all right, now."

She was probably only about three or four years old. Her dripping hair and sopping clothes were soaking Pete with smelly, brown, pond water, but Pete didn't notice. He rocked the child in his arms crooning comforting words into her wet, muddy hair oblivious to everything.

Gradually, shouting voices brought him to his senses.

"Melissa, Melissa, where are you?"

Pete jerked around. The shouting people must be looking for the little girl he was holding. She opened her eyes and stared with round, frightened, blue eyes directly into Pete's own brown ones. He stopped rocking her, smiled reassuringly at her, and asked in a quiet voice, "Do you feel better, Melissa?"

She nodded mutely.

A familiar voice said, "Pete, come on. We gotta get back."

Pete was horrified. He had done it again, endangered his own life and once again that of a friend, for Billy Fred had followed him.

Pete rose up off the ground and carried the little girl away from the pond's edge toward the voices still calling for her.

Billy Fred urged, "Come on, Pete. She'll be all right now. Let's go."

Setting her down on her feet Pete pointed in the direction of the voices and said, "Run that way and don't ever go near the water by yourself again. Understand?"

She nodded and treated him to a sweet smile before running off toward the voices.

The boys watched her run until she began yelling at the top of her lungs, "Mommy, Mommy, come see the angels."

Pete and Billy Fred jetted back up to their cloud hoping that no one was looking up, and also that no one was looking down.

Back on the cloud Jo Jo met them and said, "You two are lucky. I was just coming to find you when you went over the edge. Come on. By now, Lennie and Kaya have things set up for you." Then under his breath he added, "I hope."

Luckily, he was right. In fifteen minutes Pete and Billy Fred had been through treatments and were on the other side of the cloud trying to act as if nothing had happened.

Pete was still shaken by the weakness of his body and the difficulty he had experienced in breathing. It was odd he thought. Billy Fred seemed to have handled the contamination better than he had. Unlike Jo Jo, who had barely made it after his trip to Earth, Billy Fred seemed to have less trouble than Pete. Why would that be?

"Maybe, because I held that little girl," he said softly.

"Pete," he spoke to himself in his mind. "You've got to stop this. You've been lucky twice, but you can't continue this. Luck isn't something you can count on, you know."

CHAPTER 16

PETE'S WILD PLAN

"Why can't I? Lennie can help me get treatments when I need them, and gosh, don't you get it? I can't control myself. I don't choose to go help. I just go, and I can't depend on any more good luck. Now, I got to plan." Pete's voice was full of pleading as he tried to eliminate Kaya's opposition to the idea he had just sprung on his friends.

Kaya was continuing to shake her head back and forth, and the look on her face clearly said that she was unable to believe he was truly suggesting such a crazy scheme.

In an effort to defend himself, Pete said, "Kaya, you're the one who gave me the idea. You know, with all your talk about organizing."

"But, Pete, You're not making sense. You can't plan ahead of time, because you don't know when someone is going to need help."

"Oh, sure, I know it all sounds impossible, and I don't really know exactly how to do it, but there must be some way. I thought you could help me figure out something."

"Look! Up in the sky. It's a bird! It's a plane! No, It's SUPER PETE!" Jo Jo sang out gaily.

"Hush, Jo Jo, someone will hear you," Kaya reprimanded the clowning boy.

Jo Jo's grin slipped from his face. "I'm sorry," he apologized. Then with a solemnity he rarely showed he asked, "Pete, how can you want to make trip after trip down there? After we went that one time I was sure I was going to die. Weren't you afraid?"

"Sure, I was, and that's why I tried so hard not to do it again, but after I saw that boy hit by the truck I felt so bad. I could have helped him, and no one else could—only me. And then when that little girl fell into the pond I just went. I didn't think about it at all. I just went."

Jo Jo's solemness disappeared as he quipped with laughter in his voice, "Pete Jones, you certainly do march to the beat of your own drummer."

"What do you mean by that?" asked Vonnie.

Jo Jo grinned at the pretty blonde, his almond eyes twinkling, "You know, instead of *boom, boom, boom* like the rest of us, Pete goes *rat-a-tat-tat, rat-a-tat-tat.*"

"Very funny, Jo Jo," Vonnie said scornfully.

Kaya, taking pity on the girl, explained, "You know how most people tend to conform to the rules around them. Someone who doesn't is said to march to the beat of a different drummer."

Vonnie nodded her understanding, but Pete was feeling a little bent out of shape. He said in a defensive voice, "I don't mean to be a trouble maker."

"Of course, you don't," Vonnie said kindly.

"Pete, we know that you can't help yourself. You see someone in need, and you have to help," said Kaya.

"Yeah," Pete continued to defend himself. "That's it, and like you, Vonnie, can't help flipping back your long hair and dimpling up at everyone or crying every time something causes you worry."

Kaya took it up, "Yes, and like if Jo Jo didn't make his silly wise cracks he would burst."

Vonnie frowned as Kaya continued, "And Lennie just happening to notice exactly how Nica runs the equipment. For him there's no effort. It's easy, but for the rest of us we'd have to study for hours or maybe even days."

"Say, Vonnie," a loud voice interrupted. "How do you tell a blonde . . ."

"Oh, I get it. Just like Billy Fred can't help telling his dumb blonde jokes," Vonnie did her own interrupting as Billy Fred and Lennie joined the four already sitting.

"That's right." Kaya laughed, "And why I can't help taking over and explaining everything for everyone, and organizing."

"Which brings us right back to where we started, Kaya, I need you to help me. Otherwise, one of these times I'll dive over the side, and when I get back Nica will be waiting for me."

Vonnie pleaded tearfully, "Oh, Pete, please don't do it any more, please."

Pete bit his lip and ran his hand through his black curls, "Vonnie, I thought you said you understood. I just can't help it." His voice was louder than he had intended. Guiltily he glanced around.

"What's going on, Guys?" Billy Fred demanded. "Lennie and I just got here, and we'd like to understand, too."

Lennie nodded uneasily, his small face screwed up into a look of dismay.

Kaya answered, "Pete wants us to organize a way to protect him so he can keep helping out people on Earth."

"That's stupid, Pete!" Lennie denounced Pete's plan in his soft voice.

"I know it is, but I can't help it," Pete said stubbornly.

Kaya explained all about the conversation the two boys had missed and then asked, "Lennie, would you be willing to keep running the equipment."

Pete perked up. Had Kaya thought of something?

Lennie's mouth trembled, and his eyes were troubled. He answered in an almost inaudible tone, "I don't want to, but I'd never let any of you go without a treatment if I could help it."

"I have another idea, too," Kaya said. "Couldn't you show me exactly how to do it? Then, it wouldn't always be you who had to do it."

Lennie agreed in a relieved voice, "That's a good idea, Kaya. Sure, no problem."

"You think I could learn to run the machine then?"

"Oh, it's easy," Lennie said.

"For you, yes. I'm just not real sure about me."

Pete piped up, "Kaya, you're so smart you'll probably learn it in no time."

As usual Billy Fred couldn't resist his own urges any more than Pete could. Under drooping eyelids his eyes glittered with amusement as he spoke in an informative voice, "Speaking of smart, does anyone know what you call an intelligent blonde?"

Vonnie exploded, "No, and we're having an important discussion so just go jump off a cloud."

Billy Fred merely laughed at the girl's outrage and supplied the punch line, "A golden retriever."

As ferocious as Tess at her worse, Vonnie lunged at Billy Fred.

Abruptly he stopped his laughter and put his arms up in front of his face. Peeking out from between them, he begged in a high squeak, "Please don't hit me. I'll be good."

Vonnie collapsed back down in laughter at the boy's antics. It was really impossible to stay angry at him.

"If you're through with your fooling around I would like to know if Kaya is really going to help me." Pete turned to her and asked, "Are you, Kaya?"

Grimly the girl nodded, "Yes, I will, but we have to be super organized."

Pete smiled gratefully at Kaya and relaxed. He felt like a load had been lifted from his shoulders.

"Here comes Kat. Someone should have been with her."

"I tried, but Tess and Polly were there, and Kat seemed really interested in the book she was reading," Vonnie said as she flipped her long blonde curls back with her right hand.

Pete stood up and prepared for Kat's wrath, but when the little girl reached them she looked more worried than angry. She blurted out, "Pete, Nica's looking for you."

Kaya said, "Scatter, Gang. See you later."

Pete and Kat moved together toward Nica's office.

"Thanks, Kat. We didn't mean to have a meeting without you. It just sort of happened, and Vonnie said she couldn't tell you where she was going because of Tess and Polly, and that you were busy reading, and she didn't want to interrupt you." Pete stopped to take a deep breath.

Kat replied proudly, "It's okay, Pete. I finished my chapter and then just tuned in to you guys and listened. But Polly started teasing Tess, and Tess started chasing Polly so I said, 'You two are making me sick. I'm leaving.' But then I ran into Nica, who asked if I'd seen you. I said no, but that Tess was chasing Polly."

Kat laughed gleefully, "Nica took off after them, and I came to tell you guys."

"Cool," Pete said

CHAPTER 17

KAT LISTENS

When Pete and Kat reached Nica's office he was standing in front of the entrance as if he had been waiting for them. A smile of pleasure quickly replaced the angry expression Pete had noticed from a distance away.

Nica spoke first, "Hello, you two."

Pete murmured a hello.

Kat, in her bubbly voice, announced, "I found Pete, Nica. He was off playing with some of the others, but I told him you needed him." The look she gave Nica was positively adoring.

Pete wondered how she could possibly look at the man like that. Surely, she was pretending.

Nica said, "Will you please excuse us for a moment, Kat. I need to talk to Pete privately."

Kat nodded sadly, turned, and walked away with her head down.

Good little actress Pete thought with amusement, for he was positive Kat was still hearing every word Nica was saying. It was reassuring to know that Nica did not know about Kat's unique sense of hearing. It was also a relief to see how smart Kat was. Maybe, she wasn't just a little tattletale after all.

Nica's voice broke into his thoughts, "Pete, for some reason all the kids seem to like you."

Pete stared innocently at the handsome man's one flaw, his scar. He would concentrate on that. He would use it to remind him not to trust anything the man said, not even flattering things.

Nica continued smoothly, "You know the little boy, Gene. He is a problem. He hardly associates with anyone, merely wanders around by himself. I was wondering if you would take him under your wing. Help him become more sociable."

Pulling his eyes off the jagged scar he looked Nica in the eyes and asked boldly, "Why do you want me to?"

"I hoped you understood by now, Pete. I want you all to be happy. That is a must before we go on to the new place. We must all become one, big, happy family. Until then we cannot proceed."

Pete grimaced, "How could he fight talk about some future mumbo jumbo that Nica was most likely making up? A feeling of dejection swept over him. How could they ever find out anything about this evil man's plans for them? And even if they did, what could they do about it?

He trained his eyes back onto Nica's scar. He would not let himself be sucked into the man's lies. Pete chose his words carefully, "I don't think I'm all that popular. Just ask Brice. But if you think Gene needs help from me, I'll try."

Nica smiled hugely, "Thank you, Pete, and don't underestimate yourself."

Pete shrugged his shoulders.

"Why don't you go look for him now? I need to get on with my work," Nica said and disappeared.

Pete saw him pop up in front of the building used for producing the cloud material. Jez-beel was standing there with him. How Pete wished he could hear them! He wanted to know real bad what they were saying. He thought of Kat and turned around to search for her.

She was heading straight toward him.

He spoke softly when she reached him. "Nica and Jez-beel are over there. Will you listen to what they're saying?"

"Okay," she agreed.

Pete said, "Let's walk away from them, so they won't suspect anything."

Pete was silent as they walked. He didn't want Kat to miss a thing.

"Rats," Kat exclaimed after a few minutes.

Pete asked, "What is it, Kat?"

"I thought I'd really hear something, and then all of a sudden Nica told Jez-beel that they'd better talk later in his office."

Disappointed Pete asked, "So you didn't hear anything important at all?"

"Well, I heard something weird about experiments."

"What?" Pete demanded. "What about experiments? Tell me everything you can remember."

Kat screwed up her face as she tried to remember, "Jez-beel said something like when are you going to start the experiments? Then Nica said it had only been a month, and Jez-beel said if they're going to change won't it have happened already? Then Nica said that it takes a while for the trans—trans . . ." Kat stumbled over the word she was trying to repeat, "transfor . . . Oh, Pete, I can't remember the word."

"That's all right, Kat, maybe we can figure it out if you remember the rest of it."

She tried again, "Nica said that it takes a while for whatever that word is to take place. Then he said something about the change being gradual. Jez-beel asked if they couldn't up the dosage. Then, in a really rough voice, Nica said that it would be too dangerous."

"Is that all?"

"Not quite. Jez-beel asked how long it would be before the experiments would begin, and that's when Nica said that they had better talk later. That's all."

"Gee whiz," Pete blew air out his mouth along with his words.

"What do you think that means, Pete?" Kat asked with an anxious expression.

"I don't know, but I don't like the sound of it."

Kat's anxious expression remained as she whispered, "It's scary, isn't it?"

Yes, Kat, it is." Pete ruffled her hair in an effort to comfort her, "But don't worry. We'll all stick together, and maybe we can come up with something. Anyway, thanks heaps for listening. You've been a great big help."

The girl's face continued to be troubled, and Pete was worried about her. Would she be able to keep from telling what she had just learned?

"Listen, Kat, you won't tell anyone about what you heard, will you?"

Her troubled eyes blazed with indignation, "Of course not. I'm not as big a blabber mouth as you think."

"Hey, Kat, stay cool." Pete grinned at her. He added sincerely, "I'm sorry. I know you won't tell anyone."

CHAPTER 18

TAKING ACTION

Pete knew he shouldn't be so proud of himself, but he was happy about the way things had been going. Kaya's plan had been quite simple, but he never would have come up with it himself. He wasn't clever enough. Good thing Kaya was.

She had made a schedule for everyone to be available to sidetrack the three adults and run the treatment equipment when Pete made trips. She had also limited times for Pete to watch the Earth and made him promise not to do it at any other time.

Everyone had helped a lot. That is, everyone who knew about it—Kaya and Vonnie, Billy Fred and Jo Jo, Kat and Lennie.

Kaya had them rotating their positions so often surely no one would become suspicious of them.

Pete had also become used to the feeling of contamination from his trips to Earth. They didn't scare him nearly as much as they had. He had come to accept them like he had the colds and sore throats he used to have. Luckily, too, there had been no problems getting the treatments quickly, thanks to the close teamwork of his friends.

They had scouted around and found the perfect location for him to leave and return to the cloud. It was a secluded spot just behind the treatment room. Vonnie kept it camouflaged with some of the cloud material. If they were careful, surely no one would discover it. Sometimes, he felt like a real life Clark Kent slipping into a telephone booth to change into Superman.

Pete had been working very hard on moving his body quickly through the air. He worked at it every day, and he could now go so fast it almost seemed as if he disappeared into thin air just like the three adults. Now, he was less worried about being seen leaving or returning to the cloud.

He was happier than he had been since landing in this strange place. In the past couple of weeks he had helped a poor dog caught in a cruel leg trap, pulled a man from a burning car after an accident, and helped a rescue team find a man who had hit his head and broken some bones when he fell from a cliff.

That time had been tricky. He ended up calling for help and then disappearing before help reached the top of the cliff. He had hung around out of sight until two men spotted the injured man which, luckily, wasn't but a couple of minutes. Sometimes, Pete almost chuckled aloud when he thought about that trip. The men who rescued the unconscious man must have wondered how he could have possibly yelled for help in a kid's voice.

Pete stood up and stretched. He had been on the lookout for trouble below for about half an hour, and it was time to go show his face to the others. Kaya had been insistent about him not disappearing for more than thirty minutes at a time. Wouldn't do to be away by himself too often. Nica would be sure to notice. They had also been careful to make sure the half hour segments were at a variety of times.

He moved away from their selected, rescue site and headed toward the game room. He waved to Billy Fred and Lennie who seemed to be casually involved in conversation. They were actually keeping track of Pete to make sure he wasn't in need of a treatment.

When he reached the room he saw Gene standing off by himself. Several times he had tried to talk to Gene, but the boy remained aloof from him and the others. He tried again.

"Hi, Gene," he greeted with a smile.

Gene glanced shyly at him and mumbled, "Hi, Pete." He quickly shifted his gaze to his feet.

"How about a game of pool before we have to go to work?" Pete asked in a friendly voice.

Gene looked up at him with wary eyes under his shaggy mop of black hair and shook his head back and forth.

Pete decided to try a more direct approach, "Gene, don't you like people at all?"

That was not any better. The boy bolted without so much as a word and disappeared behind the large game room.

What a strange kid Pete thought and went into the game room. He was dismayed to find Brice, Rusty, and Owen. Only Owen took any notice of his arrival. The other two seemed to be entranced in the video game they were playing.

"Well, Pete, old pal, what have you been doing with yourself lately?" Owen asked, a fake smile on his face and a cunning gleam in his eyes.

Pete stretched his arms high above his head and began stretching his body back and forth as if working out kinks. "Oh, I've just been hanging around doing nothing."

"I see. Is there anything I can do for you?" the handsome boy asked.

Pete replied with his own question, "What do you want, Owen?"

With an innocent expression Owen said, "Why, Pete, I'm hurt. why would you think I want anything?"

"You're being rather too nice, Owen. You must want something."

"Well, now that you mention it, I was wondering how you always manage to get the girls to hang around with you so much of the time. You know what I mean?"

"Must be my good looks. It certainly isn't my money," Pete tried to joke.

Owen's innocent expression shifted into a calculated look. Glancing over at the two still engaged in their noisy game Owen pulled Pete further away and said in a confidential voice, "You know, Pete, maybe, you and I could make a little deal."

"What in the world are you talking about, Owen?"

Owen raised his eyebrow for all the world like Nica did and smiled a half smile of secret knowledge very similar to Jez-beel's favorite expression. Pete was repulsed. What was the guy up to?

Owen continued in a low voice, "Well, you're a pretty popular guy and I, my friend, have a good head for profitable schemes."

"You're nuts!" was Pete's comment. "What is there to profit from in this place?"

"See, you do need me. Why, you don't even see what could be yours with the right strategies."

"What could be mine?" Pete asked curiously.

"You, my friend, have the right charisma for running this place, but you don't have the know-how or the drive. See what I mean?"

"No. Nica runs this place, and I don't think he wants a partner."

Owen wasn't the least bit perturbed at Pete's sarcastic tone. He went on, "Well, sure, but you could run the kids here any way you wanted as long as you didn't step on Nica's toes, so what do you say? Want to form a partnership? You, the front guy. Me, the idea man."

"You are nuts!" Pete said roughly, moved away from the offensive boy, and left.

"What a jerk!" he muttered to himself.

CHAPTER 19

TROUBLE IN WICHITA

Gesturing wildly with his hands Pete related Owen's proposal to his friends. He finished with an indignant question. "Can you imagine the nerve of that guy?"

"I'm afraid Owen's one of those guys who doesn't care about anything but feathering his own nest," Kaya commented.

"Must be a vulture's nest," Jo Jo cracked

"That reminds me," Billy Fred said and looked out from under droopy eyelids at the blonde girl sitting across from him. "Vonnie, what do you call a blonde with a parrot?" he asked in a teasing voice.

'I don't know, and I don't care," was Vonnie's answer, though her voice sounded more agitated than uninterested.

"One birdbrain talking to another," Billy Fred shouted and collapsed onto the cloud in noisy laughter.

"I'll brain you one of these days, Billy Fred," the girl threatened.

"I can hardly wait," retorted the laughing boy."

"Don't worry. Be happy," Jo Jo advised with an impish grin and twinkling eyes.

The corners of Vonnie's mouth turned up into a matching grin as she conceded, "I give up. You two are never serious, and I might as well get used to it."

"If you want serious stick with Pete. He's much too serious," Billy Fred said.

"I am not!" Pete denied.

At that, they all laughed.

Kaya said, "Don't you spend all your time thinking about the bad things happening on Earth?"

"Not all my time, I don't," Pete replied, but he had to admit to himself that his life revolved around the times he could watch for troubles below.

Pete ran his finger through his kinky, black curls as he confessed, "I know you're right. I just can't help it."

"It's okay, Pete. We understand," Vonnie assured him.

Kaya added, "Of course, we do, and Pete, we're all proud of you. At least, I am, and I'm pretty sure everyone else is, too. It's awesome what you're doing to help those poor people down there."

They all agreed with her. Billy Fred added, "If you need help, I'll go with you any time."

Vonnie looked sad, and tears were brimming in her eyes. She sniffed them away and said, "Oh, Pete, I wish I could say that too, but I'd be so afraid."

"It's okay, Vonnie. No need for all of us to do dumb, stupid things. I'm really grateful for what you do to help me get treatments and all." Pete's voice tapered off into a self-conscious tone which went along with the self-conscious smile he had on his face.

Vonnie brightened, "Thank you, Pete, and you know what? I've learned how to run the treatment equipment, too. It's kind of complicated, but Lennie's such a good teacher. He's going to let me do it the next time to make sure I really can remember all the steps."

Lennie beamed at the compliment, and Pete was touched that the girl would go to all that trouble to learn. Hope welled up inside him. Even if he had to stay up here forever, maybe, they could make a difference in some people's lives below. Not as good as being back down there, but it would have to do.

Ugly thoughts broke through his good ones. What did Nica have in mind for them? Would the experiments start soon? And the worst question of all. Would they soon be swept away from this cloud to some distant spot where they could no longer have any sight of Earth?

No answers to the difficult questions came to Pete's mind.

Kaya announced, "Okay, gang, it's time for Pete's next watch. Let's go."

Everyone scattered to their assigned places.

Pete zipped behind the treatment center and into his camouflaged hiding spot. He gazed down. Surprise flooded his mind for directly below was a large city. Pete strained his eyes as hard as he could. A feeling of familiarity crept over him. Was it just wishful thinking, or was that his old neighborhood almost directly below him? What a silly thought? How would he possibly recognize it anyway from way up here?

He couldn't shake the feeling that Wichita was below them. He wished Jo Jo, with his much keener eyesight, was here. Pete saw what he thought were two tiny figures sitting on the steps of a building. He couldn't stand it. He raced to find Jo Jo.

Shortly the two boys were back behind the treatment room looking down. Pete asked anxiously, "Are there any street signs you can read, Jo Jo?"

"One at the corner says Apple," the smaller boy answered.

"Are you sure? You're not just making that up, are you?"

"Why would I do that?"

"Oh, I don't know. Can you tell me anything about the two sitting on the steps?"

"Sure. What do you want to know?"

"Does one of them look like me?"

"Well, they're both black if that's what you mean?"

"No, that doesn't help."

"I can see the number of the house across the street. It's 1204. That help any?"

Pete was stunned. Their apartment building was 1205. Was it possible that right below was his old home?"

Numbly he replied, "I think that's where I used to live."

Jo Jo sat up abruptly and said, "Confucius say, one who has lived on cloud can never live again on Earth."

Disgustedly Pete replied, "Even I know Confucius was Chinese— not Japanese."

"Doesn't matter," Jo Jo said, grinning, "I just made it up, anyway. Thought it would make more of an impression on you if you thought it came from some old philosopher."

"Would you go home if you could, Jo Jo?" Pete asked seriously. With a tragic sigh the boy replied, "Yes, I sure would."

Pete remembered that the Japanese boy had once told him he had been tricked by Jez-beel, too. He asked, "Jo Jo, how did Jez-beel get you to come with her?"

Jo Jo answered, "Well, I'd been playing basketball with my tall brother and some other friends."

Pete interrupted, "What do you mean your tall brother."

"I was adopted. So was my brother, but he's not oriental like me. He's a tall, white kid."

Pete looked puzzled.

Jo Jo explained, "My folks, that is, my adopted folks, couldn't have any kids of their own, so they adopted some. Four of us altogether, two boys and two girls. Both my sisters are part Vietnamese."

Pete nodded thoughtfully, "Go on."

Jo Jo continued, "Well, back to that night. I was getting kidded because I wasn't doing too well against the taller kids. Anyway, I ran off in a huff and ran straight into Jez-beel. Well, she was nice to me and the others were watching, and, well, it made me feel good since she was so beautiful and all. I know it sounds like a lame excuse, but she said she would show me something really special. To make a long story short I went with her, and here I am."

"I'm sorry, Jo Jo."

"Yeah, man, well, so am I."

Pete looked back over the side. For some reason they seemed to be hovering over this same spot. The two figures were still sitting on the steps. Pete said, "I'm going down, Jo Jo."

"No, don't do it, Pete. You might not be able to stop yourself from saying something if it's someone you know."

"No, I promise, I won't. I'll stay on the side of the building and listen. They won't see me."

Not giving Jo Jo a chance to stop him Pete plunged over the side and was almost instantly beside the ugly, old building which looked even more familiar now that he was close to it. A deep longing welled up inside. How he wished he could still call it home! Swallowing hard he moved closer to the front and peeked around the corner.

The deep longing grew as he recognized his oldest brother, Justin, and a boy with an abundance of long, sausage curls springing out in all directions. Pete recognized Mop, too. He and Justin had been friends for a long time.

Justin spoke, and Pete swallowed hard again. The sound of the familiar voice dredged up a flood of memories.

Pete listened to the conversation, hungry for the sound of his brother's voice. However, it wasn't long before he wished he hadn't heard a word.

The other kid said, "Justin, you got to come. The Panthers need you, Man."

"I don't know, Mop, you know how upset my mom's been ever since Pete disappeared."

"Duh! Just don't tell her anything about it, Dopey," Mop said in a disgusted voice and shook his head causing his sausage curls to bounce around.

Justin replied, "Don't call me Dopey, Dumbo. It's just that if I got stuck or plugged she'd find out for sure, and she'd take it hard."

"Come on, Man. You afraid?" Mop taunted in a high pitched whine.

In an imitation of the other boy's high, whiny voice Justin denied the implication, "No, Man, I ain't afraid."

"Okay, then, it's settled. The fight'll start at eight o-clock. Man, it'll be great giving them Vikings a thrashing. Them white dudes think they're something. We'll show 'em."

Pete cringed at the hatred and violence in Mop's voice.

It didn't look like Justin was too sure about the whole thing. His expression was solemn. Was he still thinking about how his mother would feel if anything happened to him?

Justin asked, "Kind of risky, isn't it? Taking them on before dark."

"Yeah, but it'd be risky to fight 'em in the dark, not being able to see who's who. Besides, where we going won't be nobody around to bother us."

"You sure about that? Doesn't take long for cops to get wind of things."

"I ain't worried. You worried?"

Justin looked rather worried, but he didn't admit it. He merely said, "What's to worry about?"

Mop shook his head back and forth, and the black curls bounced crazily once again. In a cheerful voice he said, "Man, we only got a few hours. You got your sharp thing?" he asked as he pulled from his pocket an oblong object. Pete gasped as an evil-looking blade shot out from one end of it.

"Yeah, sure, got it in my pocket," Justin didn't sound too enthusiastic.

Mop seemed to have enough enthusiasm for them both as he hopped up. In an excited voice he said, "Hey, maybe, we can find some rods and have us a real fun time."

Justin gave him a withering look and changed the subject. "You sure we got a ride out to that place?"

"Yeah, Man. We meet the gang at seven thirty, pile into cars, and away we go. Wheeeeeee."

Pete thought he sounded like a little boy playing with toy cars. Too bad he wasn't.

"How far did you say this spot was?" Justin asked, much to Pete's relief, for he desperately wanted to know where the fight would take place.

We take that old highway a mile east of that old, deserted warehouse on the southeast side of town. Then we turn south about a mile and a half. Then take a dirt lane kind of down into a pasture. Nothing but wide open space there. Perfect!"

"Yeah, perfect." Justin echoed the words but not the attitude.

"Come on, Justin. Let's go hang out till time to meet the gang," Mop urged.

Justin stood up, and the two began walking in the opposite direction from where Pete was hiding.

Pete started to round the corner. He had to stop his brother from getting involved with a gang fight.

CHAPTER 20

VONNIE MUST HELP

Two hands grabbed Pete's arm and held on tightly. Pete stiffened with fright until he heard a frantic voice protesting, "You can't, Pete. You know you can't."

Angrily Pete replied, "Wanta bet, Jo Jo?" He pulled away from the smaller boy, but by the time he had freed himself Justin and Mop were almost out of sight.

Jo Jo spoke, "Pete, use your head. You don't have all that much time left before you have to have a treatment. Come on, let's get back."

He knew Jo Jo was right. Sadly, Pete lifted himself up off the ground and zipped back up to the cloud.

He wanted to be angry at Jo Jo for stopping him but knew he couldn't be. He followed Jo Jo around to the front of the treatment room where Kat was bouncing up and down like a jack-in-the-box. In a dramatic voice she whispered, "Hurry up, get inside, before someone comes."

As Pete waited his turn for a treatment, his mind whirled. He had to think of a way to make sure Justin wasn't hurt in that gang fight. Not only for Justin's sake but also for his mother's sake. He could not bear to think about how sad she would be if anything happened to Justin.

Once again Kaya's planning worked well. The treatments went smoothly. True to her word Vonnie moved the switches and pushed the buttons. Lennie was at her side watching intently. Kaya and Billy Fred made sure the three adults were kept away from the treatment room, and Kat stood guard outside.

When Pete stepped out of the booth he said sincerely, "Thanks, Vonnie. You did great."

Then they scattered.

Pete raced around and around the cloud trying to calm himself down. His mind would not be calmed. He had only a couple of hours to think of a way to help his brother. What could he possibly do?

"Pete, come on. We'll be late, " a voice hollered at him.

It was Kaya. They were both scheduled to help Jez-beel. He joined her, and together they dashed to their work station.

Pete hated to work with Jez-beel worse than anything else he had to do. Usually she hovered around him, smirking and saying things about how lucky they all were to be here. A bunch of bull.

However, for some unexplainable reason she was leaving him alone. He and Kaya were able to talk as they applied the strange cloud material on top of the shelters. Pete explained about his trip and the gang fight.

"What can I do, Kaya, I mean, to help Justin?"

She frowned and replied, "Oh, Pete, you're asking for too much this time. There's no way to get the cloud back over Wichita."

Pete was discouraged. No telling how far away they were by now.

When they finished their work and were well away from Jez-beel, Pete asked Kaya, "Please, can we at least meet and try to come up with something?"

She nodded half-heartedly, and they started looking for the others. Before long they settled themselves comfortably onto the cloud's surface. The only one missing was Billy Fred. He had been involved in a pool match with Owen, Rusty, and Brice.

Pete had sent him a secret signal and hoped Billy Fred would be able to join them soon.

This time Kaya decided they should stay in the open. Disappearing together too often might arouse suspicions.

Pete could hardly stand it. He pleaded, "Kaya, can't you think of something?"

She shook her head sadly, "Pete, no matter what we do there's a good chance we'd be caught. I mean, first of all, we'd have to find a way to get the cloud back over Wichita. That would be difficult enough, but then we would have to think of some way to convince two gangs not to fight. Not to mention getting the treatments done in time."

With a heavy sigh Pete agreed, "Sounds pretty impossible, doesn't it."

The others sat mutely. Even Jo Jo remained silent.

Finally, Lennie, looking and sounding reluctant, said in his soft voice, "I can't think how it would help, but I've watched Nica move the cloud."

Pete asked, a slight glimmer of hope returning, "You think you could get the cloud exactly over the place we need to be?"

Lennie asked, "Do you know exactly where the fight will take place?"

Pete sat up straight, "Yeah, I do."

Lennie replied, "Then, I'll bet I could do it."

Pete turned quickly to Kaya, "Any way we could get Nica away from the controls for, oh say, a half hour?"

The girl frowned, "I suppose so, but would a half hour be enough time to do any good."

"If we timed it right, it might be, maybe. Don't you think so, Lennie?"

"We could get the cloud going pretty fast, but someone might notice."

"Shouldn't matter unless it was Nica who noticed. Anyone else would think it was his doing."

Jo Jo piped up, "So what are you going to do once you get the cloud over the fight?"

Pete felt as deflated as a popped balloon, "I don't know. How about raining on them? Would that work?"

Kaya said, "I don't think so. There's not as much moisture in the cloud stuff as there was when you made it rain."

She added, "Now, first things first. I think we could get Nica away if Kat would help us out."

"I'll help. Just tell me what to do." The girl's black eyes glittered with excitement.

Pete was touched. He said, "Kat, I would sure appreciate it."

Kat said, "That's okay, Pete. I wouldn't want all those kids to hurt each other."

Pete nodded his agreement. "What do you have in mind, Kaya?"

"Well, it's like this. Maybe, Billy Fred and I can get into a heated disagreement. Then, Kat can go tell Nica, and he would come to settle things."

"Do you think you could keep him there a half hour?"

"I can't promise, but we could try. Billy Fred's pretty good with words and . . . Oh, I know, maybe Kat could keep listening, and when it looks like Nica is trying to leave she can come and tell him about someone else having problems. What do you think?"

"Sounds good, and maybe, Jo Jo or Vonnie could stand outside the control room to help out if needed."

"Okay, so now we're over the place for the fight. What then?"

No one uttered a sound. They all sat as if struck with dumbness.

At last Pete groaned, "I don't know what to do."

Vonnie said, "Do you think we could make some kind of sign on the cloud? You know, like sky writing?"

Kaya looked thoughtful, "Something like, don't fight."

Jo Jo interjected, "How about, be a lover not a fighter."

The others groaned.

Just then Billy Fred arrived. He plopped down and said merrily, "Hi, Gang. Hey, anyone know who would hit the ground first if a blonde and a brunette jumped off a cloud?"

He looked around at his audience, all of whom seemed to be thinking hard."

Vonnie muttered, "Who cares?"

As usual Billy Fred quickly supplied the punch line. "The brunette. The blonde would have to stop and ask for directions."

Kaya jumped up excitedly, "That's it! That's it!"

They stared at her in bewilderment.

"Don't you get it?"

They didn't.

"Well, the Panthers are black, and the Vikings are white. Right?"

Pete agreed, "Yeah, so?"

Suddenly, it dawned on him. "Oh, I see. And guess what? All the Vikings bleach their hair or part of their hair blonde."

He turned and looked at the blonde girl who was staring at him in bewilderment.

Kaya was also gazing at Vonnie. She addressed her in a most urgent voice, "Vonnie, you have to help."

CHAPTER 21

CAUGHT

Everyone was ready.

Pete was waiting nervously a short distance from the control room. He was trying to visit casually with Lennie, but he kept glancing over at the closed door and wondering. Would Kat be able to draw Nica away from the control room? Could Lennie really get the cloud where it belonged? Most of all would Vonnie have the courage to go through with her part of the plan?

Time and again his nervous hand swept through his kinky curls. Finally, he hooked his thumbs on his pockets and was determined to keep them there.

At last it was time. Kat came bounding up to the closed door yelling excitedly, "Nica, Nica, come quick. They're fighting. Oh, please, come help."

The door flew open before Kat had a chance to knock. Nica said in his pseudo-nice voice, "Calm down, Kat, so you can tell me what is going on."

Kat did not calm down. She continued her jumping up and down. "Nica, it's awful. I need your help."

A look of impatience flashed across the man's face but was immediately replaced with his practiced smile, "Is it that important? I'm really quite busy."

Pete was pleased that Kat was able to keep up with her pretence. The little girl grabbed Nica's hand and pleaded, "Please, Nica, they're my good friends. I'm afraid one of them will get hurt."

"All right, but let's hurry." The two left.

Lennie and Pete moved swiftly to the building and through the door of the control room.

Pete whispered, "Good luck, Lennie. I'll go get . . ."

But before he could finish saying he was going to go get them, Vonnie and Jo Jo rushed through the door.

Pete breathed a sigh of relief. He hadn't been totally convinced that Vonnie would come. Even now he noticed that she had a very worried look on her very pale face.

"It will be all right, Vonnie. I'll be with you the whole time."

She didn't say a word, but she did nod slightly as if agreeing with his words.

Lennie positioned himself in front of a table covered with switches, buttons, and lights. It had to be some sort of control board. On the wall behind it was a large screen. Lennie pushed something on the control board, and the screen lit up.

Pete stared in astonishment at the images on the screen. He hoped it made sense to Lennie.

Jo Jo jarred him out of his staring. "We can handle this, Pete. You and Vonnie go do your part."

Pete opened the door and peeked out. He didn't see anyone. He said over his shoulder, "Let's go, Vonnie."

The two moved out of the door and behind the treatment room as fast as they could move. They ducked down into the hidden shelter and sat on the edge of the cloud.

It was amazing. In no time at all Lennie had the cloud positioned over the location Pete had carefully mapped out for him. Far below them, Pete could see small figures moving around in an open field. Suddenly, the figures seemed to be motionless.

Pete asked, "Vonnie, can you tell what's going on?"

"No," she answered in a quiet and rather unsteady voice.

As he continued to watch, knowledge of what was happening and what was about to happen sprang up crystal clear into his mind. The two gangs were facing each other hurling insults and challenges. Any moment they would begin fighting.

Pete grabbed Vonnie's hand and dragged her off the cloud. They dropped down quickly and screeched to a stop a little above the empty space between the two warring gangs.

Pete yelled loudly, "Stop your fighting!"

His voice did not seem to make the slightest dent in the noise being made by the screaming teenagers."

Vonnie leaned over and shouted into his ear, "I'll yell with you."

Together the two moved down to just out of reach of any grabbing hands and hollered, "Stop your fighting. Stop your fighting."

At last, a figure turned his face upward. What a sight! The face froze in wonderment. Then, like a dam bursting from too much pressure, he suddenly began shouting, "Look! Hey, look, up in the sky."

One by one, faces began looking upward. The yelling stopped, and it was now breathlessly quiet. Not one sound was coming from the stunned figures. Hands holding knives, pipes, and other weapons hung motionless as if paralysed. The moment seemed frozen in time.

Vonnie yanked on Pete and motioned to him to move up a little further from the sea of faces. She whispered in a shaky voice, "What if someone shoots at us?"

Her fear was justified for at that moment something came hurtling at them. Not a bullet, but a heavy pipe. They easily moved out of the way, but then lots of the figures below began throwing things at them.

The two hovering in the air dodged up and down and over until Pete became agitated and yelled, "Got anything else you'd like to throw?"

The gang members below lapsed into silence once again, looking up with expressions of fear and awe.

Pete continued shouting in an angry voice, "Okay, Wise Guys, if you're out of ammunition maybe you'll listen. What good's it gonna do you to hurt each other? Think it'll make you big shots? Well, it won't. All it'll do is get you thrown in jail or sent to the hospital or even worse. You ever know what it's like to be dying? Well, I do, and I don't think it's what you want. You know, maybe, some of you might do something really important some day. How are you gonna do that if you don't live long enough?"

Pete ran out of steam. Besides, he didn't have any real idea about what to say. He took a deep breath and added the only thing he could think of. "Stop your fighting! It isn't worth dying for, and it doesn't give you any points where it really counts. I guarantee that! Now, use your brains. The Panthers and Vikings can get along. Find a way."

Vonnie was shaking, but she found enough voice to agree with Pete's message, "Yes, you can find a way. Work with each other. Learn about each other. Skin isn't important. What's inside a person is the important thing. Find out what's inside yourselves and inside each other."

A familiar voice floated up from the middle of the crowd, "Pete, is that you? Are you dead?"

Justin's voice! Of course, he would recognize his own brother.

Pete didn't know how to answer Justin's questions. He was saved from doing so when several of both gangs unfroze and began shouting and running.

Chaos prevailed for a few minutes as figures ran for vehicles.

In an excited voice Vonnie shouted, "We did it, Pete! Now, we'd better get back."

Pete ignored her and intently watched the scene below.

Finally only one figure was left—his brother, Justin.

Tears came to Pete's eyes. He wanted to go down and talk to his brother, tell him . . ."

"Come on, Pete. Let's go," Vonnie urged as she pulled on him.

Justin's eyes seemed to be searching Pete's face.

Pete yanked his hand away from Vonnie's. He moved closer to Justin. He didn't know what he was going to do, but he had to say something.

Justin stood as lifeless as a statue.

"Justin, tell Mom I'm all right," Pete said in an anxious voice.

It must have been a very frightening thing for Justin. With eyes as wide with fear as any Pete had ever seen Justin came to life and bolted. He ran as if his life depended on it, and he didn't look back.

Sadly, Pete watched his brother run. He understood Justin's fears, and it was probably for the best.

He looked upward to find Vonnie waiting. At the look of pure panic on her face he came to his senses. He, at least, had to get Vonnie safely back up on the cloud. He grabbed her hand and pulled her swiftly back up to their hidden shelter.

After they landed Pete released Vonnie's hand and said, "Thank you, Vonnie."

She nodded mutely and started off. Pete followed, but the two only got as far as the corner of the treatment room when Jez-beel barred their way.

They were caught!

CHAPTER 22

DESERTED

Jez-beel smiled her secret, knowing smile and said in a low, syrupy voice, "And what have you two been up to?"

Pete tried to remain calm.

Vonnie was shaking uncontrollably, and tears were now pouring down her cheeks.

Contemptuously Jez-beel spat out at Vonnie, "Don't be such a crybaby."

She looked at Pete and treated him to her unpleasant smile and said, "I'm waiting."

"What makes you think we've been up to anything?" Pete asked in an attempt to sidetrack her. His mind was busy trying to come up with some way to get rid of the lady, so that he and Vonnie could get their much needed treatments.

But it was not to be. A whole crowd of people were approaching, and unfortunately Nica was one of them. In fact, Nica was dragging Lennie with one hand as the boy clutched the crutches he refused to give up. Jo Jo was with them, and not far behind were Kaya, Billy Fred, and Kat.

There was no sign of the pleasant, friendly Nica. This man was angry and ugly with a scowl of hatred etched upon his face.

"I demand to know what is going on," he directed the words at Pete as if he already knew who was responsible.

Pete sought out Kaya's eyes. She shrugged her shoulders slightly and looked as if she wanted Pete to know something, but Pete couldn't figure out what was in her mind. He knew he couldn't let his friends be blamed for what he had caused so he spoke out in what he hoped was a strong voice, "It's all my fault, Nica."

"I was certain of that, Pete. What I am not certain about is the extent of the situation."

Deciding that complete confession was the only way out he told about the trip to Earth. Then he begged, "Please, can't you let Vonnie have a treatment? I made her go. It's not her fault."

Nica turned angrily to the girl, "Is that true, Vonnie? Did he force you to go contaminate yourself?"

Vonnie's tears had not let up, and she was slumping as if she didn't have enough strength to keep herself upright. Her voice was weary. "He needed me to go so they wouldn't hurt each other."

Nica turned his anger back upon Pete. "How dare you! How dare you defy me! You have used up your last chance. Now, you will suffer the consequences for your actions."

Pete knew he was doomed. He felt his breaths coming in shorter, faster gasps as he tried to take in the oxygen he needed.

"I understand, Nica, but Vonnie, please. She needs a treatment."

But Nica ignored his words. He had turned away toward Jez-beel. "Send Sadju over and get ready to vacate this place."

Jez-beel disappeared.

Nica turned back. "We're leaving, Pete. Not you, however. I think you understand why."

Pete made himself look the man in the eyes, and he replied, "All right." He felt it truly didn't matter as long as Nica was taking Vonnie with the others. He deserved to be left, but she didn't. Pete allowed himself to collapse onto the cloud.

Soon Sadju, as well as the rest of the children, joined them.

Nica turned to the group and said loudly, "We are leaving this place. That is," he paused and made a sweeping look over them. "That is, if you choose to go."

How could they ever have believed his smile was pleasant? Now, it looked as evil as ever evil could look and was directed at Vonnie who was lying on the cloud.

Pete knew without a doubt that Nica was leaving her, too.

Although he felt he could no longer make his body do what he wanted, Pete's mind was still working just fine—much too fine. It might be better if he could slide into unconsciousness. Then he wouldn't have to face up to what he had done to Vonnie.

The girl was staring up at Nica with eyes clouded with pain and a fearful expression.

"I'm sorry, Vonnie. I'm so sorry," Pete moaned.

Nica was talking again, "Pete has taken it upon himself to expose our situation to the world below. That means we must vacate this place at once."

Pete opened his mouth to protest that they were probably as safe as they had ever been, but Nica was rapidly continuing, "We will leave in a few moments."

Nica swung around and addressed the small boy crouching by himself at the far end of the treatment room. "Gene," he said in a chilling tone, "You're ready to go on to somewhere new, aren't you?" Nica's face changed from it's hardness to a pleasant expression.

Absolute terror erupted on Gene's face. He yelled loudly, "No! No!" and ran off.

Nica turned back to the others with a frown, "What do you suppose that was all about?" he asked of no one in particular.

He looked at Pete with hatred burning in his eyes. "Pete, have you been scaring Gene?"

Pete shook his head weakly and answered, "No, Nica. Gene won't talk to me."

Flicking his hand as if it didn't matter Nica said, "What about the rest of you? If you are ready to go with me stand over by Sadju."

Immediately there was a stampede over to Sadju. However, Nica's cunning smile changed to bewilderment as he gazed over at the many kids still remaining where they had been.

Nica asked in a perplexing tone, "Kaya, surely you will go on with me. You are too intelligent to stay here and die."

"I won't go if Pete and Vonnie don't go," she said with a stubborn look on her face.

Nica's face hardened. "They are contaminated. They cannot go."

"Can't they take a treatment? Then they won't be contaminated."

"No!" he barked out in a vengeful voice. "They disobeyed."

"Well, I disobeyed, too."

"You went to Earth?" he asked with a frown.

"No, but I knew they were going."

Again he flicked his hand. "As you wish then, Kaya, but I am sadly disappointed in you."

He spoke to the others standing with Kaya, "And the rest of you? You choose to stay here, also?"

Billy Fred, Lennie, and Kat nodded.

Jo Jo chuckled and said, "I couldn't bear to leave this place. It's so much fun."

"Bah, I'm through with you," he denounced them and turned to the kids standing with Sadju. "Let's load up. Jez-beel should be ready by now. Sadju, get everyone into the bubble immediately. I will join you there in a few moments. I have something to take care of." He disappeared.

Silently, Sadju and the others moved toward the bubble's storage room.

Kaya ran toward Vonnie and Pete. "Come on, you two, let's get you into the treatment room, pronto."

Billy Fred, Jo Jo, and Kat were right behind her. Lennie had already rushed into the treatment room.

Billy Fred said, "I don't think Nica knows we can run the equipment. Otherwise, I don't think he would just leave us like this." Billy Fred leaned down to pull Pete to his feet.

Pete said in his weak voice, "Don't touch me, Billy Fred, you'll contaminate yourself."

"Doesn't matter. I'll just take a treatment, too." He grinned.

With Kaya and Billy Fred helping, Pete and Vonnie drug themselves into the treatment room. Lennie was busy fiddling with switches and buttons.

Vonnie was hastily placed into the booth. In four minutes,

when they let her out, she was as strong as ever, but she still wore the look of one caught in a nightmare.

Billy Fred pushed Pete into the booth.

Then Kaya and Billy had their turns.

When they finally finished, and everyone was back to normal, they made their way over to the bubble's storage room. As they expected it was empty. Nica had made good his threat. He and the others had left, and now they were the only ones on the cloud.

They had been deserted!

CHAPTER 23

EIGHT ALONE

Even though the deserted kids had expected to find the bubble gone, they were stunned. They stood silently staring into the empty building until, at last, Kaya asked, "Well, Guys, what now?"

Billy Fred ventured, "Well, we could always have a joke-telling contest."

Vonnie rolled her eyes and groaned.

Pete tried to smile but wasn't really in a joking mood. He said, "I wish that's all we had to do, but I think we had better do some planning if we're going to survive in this place by ourselves. What do you think, Kaya?"

"You're right, Pete. We have to take care of ourselves now. I think we had better . . ."

A figure came hurtling toward them. It was Gene.

What a surprise! They had forgotten all about the boy who had taken off when Nica had approached him about leaving the cloud.

Jo Jo teased, "It's an invasion!"

Gene did not look amused. His face remained grave, and his voice was more animated than Pete had ever heard it before. He spoke directly to Pete, "Can you help?"

He paused and seemed to be struggling for words.

Pete waited, but Billy Fred didn't, "What do you need help with?"

Gene glanced over at Billy Fred but once again spoke to Pete. "You're the one who helps, and we need help now."

Pete responded in a puzzled voice, "Sure, Gene, I'll help you. What's up?"

"There's a bomb!" he shouted in a panicked voice.

Everyone began talking at once.

Kaya shouted, "Hey, Gang, be quiet and let Gene finish."

Gene seemed to forget his shyness as he continued, "There's a bomb over there in that locked building. I thought I could get in and do something, but I've tried and tried and I can't get into the building. Please, it's going to go off in . . ." he broke off and then said, "I'm not sure exactly when but soon."

They raced over to the locked building with Pete leading the way.

After studying the lock Pete said in a defeated tone, "It looks complicated, and I think we would have to know the combination. Maybe, it would be better if we hid out on the other side of the cloud. Maybe, the blast won't be so bad over there."

"No, no, it's going to blow up the whole cloud. Nica doesn't want anything left."

"How do you know, Gene?" Kaya asked curiously.

For the first time Gene spoke to someone other than Pete. He looked scared to death, but he answered her, "Sometimes—sometimes I can tell what Nica is thinking. I don't know how, but I can. He thinks mean things. He wanted to do experiments on us to find out if we had developed any super powers. I knew I had, and I didn't want him to know I could read his mind—that I could even when I didn't want to."

"And that's how you know about the bomb? You read his mind?" Kaya asked.

He nodded his head. "Yes, yes, and I know his mind said to push A-25, C-3, T-6. But I've tried it and tried it, and it doesn't open. I gave up and came to find you because . . ." he stopped himself again and beseeched Pete with round, black eyes.

Pete waited for the boy to finish what he was going to say. He watched Gene moisten his lips.

Gene finally continued, "Sometimes, I can tell what you're thinking, too. I know you want to help other people. I know you have good thoughts."

"Oh," Pete said at the revelation and wondered if the boy could read all their minds whenever he chose to. That question would have to wait until later. That is, if there was a later—if they survived. Right now they had better try to do something about the bomb.

"Gene, what if we do get in? Do you know how to stop the bomb going off?"

The boy frowned. He answered in such a soft voice that Pete had to lean toward him in order to hear. "I thought so, but then I thought I could unlock the door." His black eyes were filled with frustration.

Another soft voice spoke up, "It's open. We can go in."

Pete jerked around and said, "How did you do that, Lennie?"

"Gene told me how," he answered and at the same time gestured with one of his crutches for them to enter.

"Why couldn't he open it then?" Billy Fred demanded as he passed the boy on his way into the building.

Lennie shrugged, "I don't know, unless it's because he doesn't know about the special code on all the equipment."

Special code?" several of the kids exclaimed together as they filed into the building.

Gene looked and sounded confused as he protested, "But I knew Nica's thinking. Why didn't I know about a special code?"

Kaya said sharply, "Worry about that later. Right now we had better do something about the bomb."

She walked over to Lennie who had been the last one to come through the doorway, "I think you're our best bet, Lennie. Think you can do it?"

"I'll try," he replied with a troubled look.

The room they were standing in was large. Pete looked around to see if he could spot anything that looked like a bomb. He asked Gene, " Do you know where the bomb is?"

"I only know that it's behind a large panel."

Pete was overwhelmed by what he was seeing. He said in awed voice, "What a strange place!"

And it was. There were several booths, all looking much like the treatment booth, as well as all kinds of other, strange-looking equipment. This must be the place where Nica had planned to do experiments on them. It looked like a place a mad scientist might create to do really weird things.

It gave Pete a creepy feeling. Deliberately he pushed such thoughts away. They had to find that bomb before it was too late. There were several panels of buttons and switches, but there was one really huge one. It was at the far end of the room.

Gene pointed at it and said, "I think the bomb is behind that big panel."

They all moved toward it. Jo Jo peeked behind it and said, "There is something back there. You look, Gene."

Gene walked behind the panel and said over his shoulder, "Yeah, that's got to be it."

"Okay, now what do we do next?" Kaya asked.

Gene came back out before answering, "If I go backwards from what Nica did I think this is what we need to do."

He stopped, wrinkled his brow in concentration, and said, "The red wire needs to be disconnected first. Then the black wire, and last of all the blue wire, but first of all we need to push all the green buttons and move the largest lever on the right side of the panel up as far as it will go." He frowned and then added, "There's only one thing I'm not exactly sure about."

Pete held his breath. Was there something so complicated they would never figure out? He was suddenly petrified. He didn't want to be blown up. Even if he had to spend forever on this cloud he didn't want that bomb to go off.

Gene said, "After setting the bomb Nica thoughts said he was pushing green buttons and pulling a large lever at the end of the control board. I don't know if he had a certain order when he was pushing the green buttons. I also don't know if you should push buttons first or pull the lever first. I'm sorry."

Pete grabbed Lennie's arm as the boy was reaching for something on the panel. "Do you have it all straight? Do you know how to push the green buttons? Do you know which to do first? The buttons or the lever?" He let go of the other boy's arm.

Lennie said with a grin, "How do you think I was able to open the locked door? There's a certain way Nica ran every thing. He probably did it so automatically he didn't have to think about it. That's why Gene didn't get a clear reading on how to do it. I'm pretty sure I push the buttons first."

Pete watched anxiously. It was all up to Lennie now. They had to trust him.

Lennie began pushing green buttons in what looked to Pete like a double figure eight, which resulted in the center button being pushed several times and all the others only once. When he finished with the green buttons he moved down to the right end of the panel and pushed a large lever up. He moved on around the end of the panel and disappeared behind it. After only a few seconds he emerged and said quietly, "I did everything Gene said to do."

Vonnie asked tearfully, "Do you think it's all right?"

Kaya didn't answer but asked her own question, "Gene, when was the bomb suppose to go off?"

"I don't know exactly. I only know that Nica thought . . ." He interrupted himself and paused as if trying to remember. Staring off into space he continued quoting Nica's thoughts. *'There, that will take care of this place and those kids. Guess I'll have to write this off as a bad venture unless there is still something I can do with the ones going with us. Wish it could have been some of the others. I think the ones staying behind had the most potential for super powers. That Brice has just become a super bully, and Tess will never be anything but a super spitfire, and Polly is a totally self-centered nothing.'* That's all I remember," Gene concluded.

He realized all the other kids had been listening and watching him. He ducked his head in embarrassment.

Vonnie, still not convinced about the bomb, repeated her earlier question in a nervous voice and asked another one, "Isn't there some way we can be sure the bomb's not going to go off?"

Diving behind the panel Pete came out carrying an innocent-looking, metal box with colored wires dangling down its sides.

Vonnie cringed at the sight of it. The others stood still and stared except for Billy Fred. He said, "What are you going to do with that thing?"

"I'm going to get rid of it."

In a concerned voice and with an even more concerned look on her face Kaya said, "Pete, you can't just throw that thing off the cloud. What if it lands somewhere and explodes?"

Pete stopped in his tracks. That was exactly what he had been planning to do. What now? The thing in his hands was making him feel extremely vulnerable.

Jo Jo said in his merry way, "Don't worry. Be happy."

Pete turned to Gene, "Do you think this thing will go off now?"

Gene answered, "No, it's disconnected. But I don't know what would happen if it hit hard on the ground."

Kat, tired of being quiet, spoke out in a cranky voice, "Hasn't it been here all the time? Why should it go off if we don't make it?"

"Out of the mouth of babes," Jo Jo said. "She's right. It's been here all the time. We'll just have to keep it."

Kaya said, "I wonder where Nica kept it. I mean, he surely didn't leave it lying around behind that panel."

Gene brightened up. "That's right. He got it out of a locked box."

"Is that it?" Kat asked pointing to a large, metal box sitting along the side of the room.

They trooped over to examine the box. Opening the lid they found it had very thick walls with a hole exactly the right size to hold the bomb.

Gently, Pete placed the bomb into the container, closed the heavy lid, moved back, and announced. "There. Now, Lennie or Gene, do either of you know how to lock this thing?"

The two boys exchanged looks, then both smiled and answered almost simultaneously, "We'll figure it out."

Pete left them to it.

CHAPTER 24

A MISSION

No more Nica. No more Jez-beel. No more Sadju. Just the eight of them all alone. Pete felt like his brain was on overload. He muttered, "I need some fresh air," and escaped from the shelter.

He would like to explore the large room full of bizarre equipment some day, but for now he just wanted to get away from it.

He needed to think. Questions were raging. What would they do now? Could they survive? Where would they go? What would they do?

Pete quickly made his way over to a place on the edge of the cloud, stretched out on his stomach, and looked down. It had turned dark long ago and all he saw below were lights flickering up at him. Looked a little to him like the stars flickering above him. What a strange world he was living in! A multitude of thoughts continued to invade his mind.

The eight of them were now totally responsible for running the equipment on the cloud—the machine that produced the cloud material, the controls which moved the cloud, and of course, the treatment room. Was it all possible?

Another thought sprang into his mind. Should they try to contact anyone on Earth and let them know what had happened to them? Could they? What if they did and then died because people insisted they come back to Earth?

Again and again these thoughts pounded at his brain until he couldn't stand to think about it any more.

He jumped up and headed for the game room. He would immerse himself in a video game and not think at all.

Pete hadn't been playing very long when the others began drifting into the game room. Soon they were all there—even Gene. No one brought up their situation. Everyone was playing games in a subdued manner.

Angrily Pete banged his hand on the side of the video game and turned around to face the other seven. The loud, metallic sound had caused them to stop what they were doing and look at him.

Jo Jo was the first to speak, "Confucius say, what we do now?"

Pete shrugged and asked his own question, "Pete say, what we do now?"

"I've been waiting for someone to ask," Kaya said. "We need to get organized. We have a cloud to run."

"Why didn't you say so before?" Pete queried.

"I didn't want you all to call me bossy," Kaya replied with a chuckle.

"I promise I won't if you promise to take over and get us organized," Pete said with his own chuckle.

Noisy agreements filled the air.

As they gathered themselves around Kaya she began explaining her ideas. "Okay, Vonnie's good at knowing exactly how to spread the material so she'll be in charge of that. For now, Lennie can decide how and where we'll move the cloud, and also I hope, show us how to run the equipment for producing the cloud stuff."

She looked questioning at the small, insignificant-looking kid.

He was standing across from her leaning on his crutches.

Strange, Pete thought, how badly they needed Lennie in order to survive up here. As he watched Lennie, the crippled boy seemed to grow taller and stronger.

He smiled happily at Kaya and then looked at Pete. "Pete, do you really think I can get along without these things?"

Pete knew he was referring to his crutches and the conversation they had had about them. He answered, "I'm sure of it."

Lennie allowed the two sticks of wood to drop and stood without wavering. He laughed aloud and kidded, "I bet now I could be the best funambulist in the world."

"Funambulist!" Kaya exclaimed. "What is that?"

Lennie laughed again. "A tightrope walker. I'll bet that now I can balance on any little, old thing."

"Cool," Pete voiced his agreement.

Kaya added hers. "Yes, I believe you could, but what about operating the equipment to made the cloud stuff?"

"Oh, sure. No problem. I watched . . ."

"Yeah, Lennie, we know, you watched Sadju once, and now you can do it easily. It's not fair to be so smart!" Billy Fred said, his hang dog eyes twinkling.

Lennie laughed even louder. "I know it, Billy Fred. I guess I'm pretty lucky, aren't I?"

What a change! Pete thought and hoped Lennie would not let it all go to his head. Right now he certainly held all the cards.

He needn't have worried. Lennie was continuing kindly, "I'll show you how to run everything, and if there's anything I don't know Gene probably can help."

Gene smiled shyly. He still didn't seem to have a lot to say, but at least he was with them and not off by himself. Maybe, eventually, he would be as noisy as the rest of them.

"That would be great, Lennie," Kaya said. Then she looked at Gene and asked, "Are you willing to help, Gene?"

"Yes, if I can, but I don't think Lennie will need any help."

Pete noticed a look pass between the two boys and realized that the two had already developed a friendship. That was good. They had a lot in common.

Now that survival was taken care of, Pete was back to worrying about his original problem—the one that had caused this situation. He asked carefully, "Kaya, what about my helping people down on Earth?"

"Well, Pete, I don't suppose we would ever be able to stop you without tying you up or locking you in one of the rooms, but you'll have to be careful. Think you can do that?"

Pete said, "I'll try, Kaya. I'll try, but do you think it would be wrong or maybe dangerous if someone did find out about us up here?"

"I don't know, but for now we had better not take any chances."

Pete nodded, "He had come to that same conclusion.

"Could we have some kind of school like we talked about?" Vonnie asked. "We have to do something in this place, or we'll be terribly bored. I was already bored,"

Kaya answered, "Of course, we can. There are lots of things we can teach each other, and we also need to learn as much as we can about everything here . . ."

Pete interrupted, "And we need a purpose in our lives. I mean, besides playing games and having a good time."

"We'll be learning to survive on our own," Lennie contributed. "That will take some doing."

Kat said, "I'm kind of scared."

Pete moved over to the little girl who had been so quiet since all of this had happened to them. He said, "Kat, we're all kind of scared. We'll have to take care of each other."

A brief smile flickered across her face, "Okay, Pete, and will you sometimes play a game with me?"

"You bet! And I'll beat you, too!" he answered and couldn't resist sweeping the child up and twirling her round and round.

Kat giggled happily, and as soon as Pete put her down she stated, "Oh no, you won't. I'll practice until I'm so good you'll never beat me."

Pete sobered up a little and said, "Back to my idea about having some purpose. I'd like our purpose to be to help as many people as we can whenever we can."

"You would," Billy Fred said, "I believe you like making secret trips to Earth."

Pete confessed, "I guess that's true, but honestly, Billy Fred, it's more than that. I can't help myself."

"Yeah, Pal, I know."

Kaya said, "'We'll put it to a vote. All those in favor of making our mission to help people in trouble dog pile Pete."

Pete was immediately pounced on by everyone. He didn't exactly see everybody hit him, but it certainly felt like all seven were on top of him. He was still laughing when the others finally let him up.

He had to pull himself up out of the cloud and brush the white stuff off.

He sobered again as it hit him that he would never be reunited with his family. He was lucky in a way, though, for now he had a new family, and he also cared about them an awful lot.

Pete studied each one as they chattered among themselves. Kat, who had reminded him so much of his little sister, Joni, and had such extraordinary hearing. Billy Fred and his constant jokes, but who was willing to go anywhere anytime to help out. Kaya, who would keep them organized. Vonnie, who, despite her terrible fears, had come through when she was needed. Jo Jo, whose vision could pick out things down on Earth that none of the rest of them could see and who was such a good friend. Lennie, whose tremendous mental abilities had saved him more than once and who would help them all survive up here; and last of all, Gene, who had come out of his shyness to save them from Nica's evil plan to blow them up.

What lay ahead for them all? It was scary, but wasn't it also exciting? For himself, he thought it could be very exciting and rewarding. But what about the others? Once again he studied their faces as they continued to chat with each other.

Billy Fred noticed his gaze, smiled mischievously, and spoke out in a voice loud enough to quiet the others, "Vonnie, what do you call a blonde with a mission?"

This time it was Billy Fred who was dog piled.

www.ingramcontent.com/pod-product-compliance
Lightning Source LLC
Chambersburg PA
CBHW070757120626
46557CB00002B/637